SUBTLE ENERGY

SUBTLE ENERGY

A HANDBOOK OF PSYCHIC ENERGY MANIPULATION

KEITH MILLER

Turtles
& Crows

Subtle Energy: A handbook of psychic energy manipulation. Second Edition.

Keith Miller.

ISBN: 978-1-7337688-0-1

To my kind teachers,
and all those who have supported me
and shown me patience

TABLE OF CONTENTS

Author's Note 1

Preface...3

A Historical Introduction to Subtle Energy............................7

A Philosophical Introduction to Subtle Energy 15

The Energy Body 25

Religion and Spirituality 29

Self-Care 35

Learning Psychic Energy Work..37

Meditation and Observation..39

Directing Energy within the Body 45

Psychometry and Imprinting 49

Grounding and Centering...57

Constructs...67

Energetic Hygiene and Dissolution...................................73

Energetic Healing and Aura Reading 77

Wards and Defensive Constructs......................................85

Communication: Telepathy and Empathy 93

Astral Projection 101

Clairvoyance 115

Working with Spirits 121

Interfacing with Magic: Thoughtforms and Servitors 129

Interfacing with Magic: Elemental Working......................135

Beyond Technique...139

Appendix A: Chakras and Energy Centers 143

Appendix B: On Hermetic Philosophy in this Book 149

Appendix C: On Alchemical Elements 155

    Elemental Modes 158

    Eastern Systems of Elements... 160

Appendix D: Psychokinesis 163

Further Reading.. 167

About the Author 169

Author's Note

When I first wrote *Subtle Energy*, I was largely working from a body of knowledge collected over many years of engagement with the online energy community and the paranormal in general. However, while that book represented the best of my knowledge at the time, I did not stop those studies. I am now happy to update this text with new information acquired over the last year of my studies, as well as with citations and sources, where available, to which the reader may refer for more information about concepts or their origins. Additionally, I have revised my treatment of certain concepts about which I may have been unduly critical.

This second edition represents a marked improvement in the presentation of information. The greatest changes are the addition of chapters on the energy body and communicating with spirits. Additionally, some exercises and concepts have been updated with the fruits of my research on psychic ability and intuition development pedagogy. Sections have been added on psychometry and aura reading, and a new chapter discusses communication with spirits. Illustrations of some concepts have been added. Centering exercises and greater details on the nature and purpose of chakras is now included. In short, I believe that the book has undergone significant improvements that merit this second edition.

PREFACE

The direct manipulation of subtle energy is a way to affect one's influence on the world and to perform a variety of psychic feats such as telepathy, clairvoyance, and so on. Though often regarded as a modern approach to magical systems, with a relatively short history, direct manipulation of subtle energies has been a part of magical practices and systems across cultures since as long as these things have been documented. What has changed—what is new to the approach in this current era – is our application of scientific, rather than spiritual or philosophical, terminology to this kind of work. Today, many people speak of manipulation of energy in modern terms, with mental imagery of waves, forces, and particles.

Another relatively recent convention is the manipulation of subtle energy as a goal unto itself. Historically in most magical systems in both the East and the West there has been an awareness and acknowledgement of subtle energy as a factor in magical work, but this has generally been regarded as a medium or mechanism by which an effect is carried out. The aim was not to manipulate the energies, but rather to bring about the desired result, with subtle energy being considered more of a medium or a vehicle than the agent of the activity. The focus on subtle energy work as a goal in and of itself is indeed a fairly modern convention, though it does not seem to be one that is going away, nor does it lack merit simply because it is new.

Still, it is important to consider why people work with subtle energy itself, what they are aiming to achieve or what they are avoiding, and how this particular work has its own benefits and shortcomings. It is the opinion, perhaps not entirely unfounded, of many magicians of the more ritualistic sort, that energy work as such is merely a shortcut, and one that tends to bring about inferior results. Energy workers answer by saying that they have merely removed the unnecessary and tedious steps of the ritual and choose to bring about the result themselves, directly. But this kind of antagonistic relationship does not need to be the case. There are applications for which subtle energy work itself is very well suited, and there are applications where it can be used to enhance or inform the sorcerer's work on either a theoretical or practical level. Energy workers and sorcerers alike would do well to learn from the other systems rather than jump into immediate criticism; after all, there is plenty to criticize based on the merits without making implicit assumptions of other people's ways of working.

I will be aiming to address with this book what I have learned in my 18 years of engagement with subtle energy manipulation, a term that has not always been consistently used but which is, I believe, the most accurate for what I will discuss. Over the years, it has been referred to as psionics, psychic energy manipulation, psychoenergetics, psi manipulation, energy work, and a number of other terms, and I've used a number of these terms myself. I have chosen to adopt the term subtle energy because it fits, without carrying with it as much baggage.

This term has its own baggage, to be sure, but it's baggage that I keep my clothes in, so to speak. "Subtle energy" addresses nicely the Hermetic concepts that I use as my working philosophical basis; it avoids overly materialistic scientific language, which I find the wrong tool for the job; and it establishes immediately a contrast between *subtle* energy and the less subtle sorts. It also avoids using terms from other fields, whereas *psychic* energy is a term of art in psychology relating to how much mental energy a person has to engage in cognitive processes (the exhaustion of which leads to the deployment of various ego defenses). So, the term subtle energy avoids the risk of confusion with other relevant fields (such as psychology), while communicating the idea succinctly of what *is* being referred to, and without being too cumbersome a term. It will suit.

I have also made an attempt with this book not to offer a
simple collection of visualization exercises intended to be served
directly out of the can. Instead, while I do offer an example
visualization or exercise from time to time, I have attempted to
deliver a description of the processes involved such that you can
develop and employ your own set of visualizations and
techniques which are meaningful to you. It is my sincere hope
that the energy worker who reads this book will come away
with a sufficient knowledge and understanding that they might
be able to not only perform the exercises and methods I
describe. Far more importantly, I hope that you come away
from this book with an understanding that allows you to
innovate and develop your own methods.

A Historical Introduction to Subtle Energy

A great number of spiritual practices from around the world allude to or directly work with some kind of subtle or psychic energy or force. Though called by many names, this energy tends to behave similarly enough throughout traditions that it is possible to study it as a thing unto itself, informed by a wide variety of traditions. It is difficult to say when the practice of subtle energy manipulation became a goal or practice in its own right, but in broad strokes it seems to be a fairly recent phenomenon. While many traditions both ancient and modern have worked with this energy, or alluded to it, or taught about it, it has rarely been the *focus* of a practice. More commonly, it is understood as either a mechanism of action, by which a ritual, spell, meditation, or so on is efficacious; or it is a means to an end, the manipulation of which is used to engage in the work of spiritual alchemy – the transformation of the self into something beyond the mundane.

As this is primarily intended as a practical text, it would be far too involved to discuss every system's understanding of subtle energy in its own terms and to them do proper justice in this work. However, if one wished to commit to another system to learn more about its approach to subtle energy, there are a great number of choices. *Chi* in the Chinese systems, as understood in the internal martial arts, or *ki* in the Japanese language and its systems, including Reiki, are well known examples of such a subtle energy. In India, there are yogic practices focusing on *prana*, or breath. Tibetans understand the body channels to be full of moving *lung*, or wind. In the scientific materialism of the Soviet Union, *bioplasma* was the term used to describe the proposed force by which psychokinesis was possible, and in the West we have long used the term *psi* for the unknown, and *psi energy* became the common term to describe this, with the CIA in its research using the term *psychoenergetics* for the entire field. In this book, I have chosen to use the term "subtle energy" as a descriptive term which does not carry with it the materialistic or scientific implications of words like "psychoenergy" or "bioplasma," nor the cultural baggage of terms like "chi" or "lung."

No matter what it's called, the general themes remain the same: subtle energy is the vehicle by which psychic or magical effects may be achieved, and the manipulation of which is a psychic discipline unto itself. However, in nearly all of the above traditions, this subtle energy is worked with only as a means to an end. Achieving control over it may only be important as a stepping stone to another, greater result; be it physical, spiritual, or mental. Indeed, often in the pursuit of spiritual paths abilities related to psychic phenomena are achieved as a matter of course, rather than as a deliberate goal. The yogi achieves miracle powers not by seeking the miracle powers, but by seeking enlightenment. Along this path, powers may be developed, but they are a side effect rather than the goal. This kind of secondary focus is very common among spiritual paths.

In other cultures, psychic ability in general is accepted as a matter of course. Tibetan culture makes no secrets about the regular use of oracles or astrology, or the influence of magical rituals in daily life. In China, as well, a belief in the paranormal is commonplace, with even important business decisions being made only after consulting an astrologer in many cases. In Japan, there is no question of the existence of *ishin-denshin*, a mutual understanding that arises through unspoken communication. The word itself means "what the mind knows, the heart transmits" and suggests the same esoteric heart transmission as is found in Tibetan Buddhism. There, the true understanding of the nature of reality cannot be communicated in words, and the understanding must instead be transmitted from the heart of the master to the student. In *Original Wisdom*, Robert Wolff described the uncanny knowledge of Malaysian aboriginal tribes. But in these cultures, psychic ability is not a goal to be strived after. Instead, it is merely a fact of living.

Even when psychic abilities are the goal, the direct manipulation of energy is not usually the aim. In trying to develop telepathy, clairvoyance, or psychokinesis, questions about *psi energy* or so on might be entertained, not because there is inherent value in such energetic work, but because of the potential abilities to which it relates. Interest in manipulating subtle energy directly as its own discipline is a fairly recent development.

The work with this energy, in the West, became very popular along with the rise of spiritualism in the 19th century and particularly with the Theosophical Society.[1] Spiritualism developed at the cusp of, or perhaps in response to, the scientific advances of the era. As it formalized in the late 1800s it became subject to far more rigorous analysis. A spiritual medium now had to produce fairly grand results to be taken seriously, and accusations of fraud amongst mediums outside of respected circles led to a sort of standardization in how things were proposed to work. Increasing scientific scrutiny led to the some of the first real scientific investigations of psychic phenomena as well as investigations into ghosts and spirit mediums generally.[2]

Around the same time, the Theosophical Society was founded in New York and took a heavy handed and imperialistic approach to seeking the "truth."[3] Perennial

---

[1] See for example Blavatsky's *The Secret Doctrine* (1888), in which she expounds on her theories in great detail, including concepts of the energy body.

[2] The focus of the Society for Psychical Research, founded in 1882, among others.

[3] With the objective of discovering the truth inherent in all religions—so called "perennial philosophy" – early Theosophists would pick and choose concepts from other cultures and religions which supported their own notions of this universal, perennial

philosophy, the idea that all spiritual practices have the same origin and so carry the same "truths," but that these "truths" were often corrupted or obscured by primitive peoples' cultures, led to the assimilation of a huge amount of occult knowledge from around the world into an unfortunately homogenized stew from which it became very difficult to extract any particularly useful information unless one was particularly keen on that paradigm.

It is this reckless approach that led to a great number of misunderstandings that remain persistent in the Western esoteric tradition today, such as the ubiquitous chakra model taken from a single misunderstood tantric source.[4] Despite the less than culturally sensitive approach (admittedly quite common and popular at the time), it is this aggressive search for "truth" by distilling the common elements of various esoteric traditions that first brought about the idea that this subtle energy may be an actually existent and important thing. After all, if so many cultures have ideas about it, then surely there must be something there.

Reflections of these Theosophical ideas are found in nearly every facet of modern mysticism or New Age spirituality. Edgar Cayce, the American clairvoyant and Christian mystic, often referred to such concepts in his life readings, where he would refer to past lifetimes spent in Atlantis, Lemuria, or so on. Along with this interest came an unfortunate support for scientific racism, following from Blavatsky's concept of "root

---

"Truth." Today's Theosophical Society maintains much of the same original framework.

[4] C.W. Leadbeater's *The Chakras* (1927), which expounds on the now generally accepted seven chakra model, was itself based on translations by Sir John Woodroffe, and make assumptions based on already established Theosophical Society beliefs of the time. The dubious quality of Woodroffe's translations, as well as their own unorthodox source, compounded into misunderstandings which are now considered orthodox.

races" and the different "strains" of humanity with different histories and capacities.

At the same time, however, a functional symbolic model and spiritual anatomy was distilled from ancient sources. The chakra model resultant from Leadbeater's is functional, though not necessarily reflected, as he purports, in any clairvoyant investigation of the energy body. Steiner's model in anthroposophy follows in the same way. Both will be found by clairvoyants who use the model, because they are a way of organizing the presence or absence of certain categories of mental activities within the astral field. However, for people who do not use that method of organizing information, they may not appear. This is an important thing to recognize.

At this point, it is difficult to conceive of other ways to organize the structure of the human energy body. The energy field as presented by the Theosophical Society and its successors is well understood and well organized, and can now be found in the Theosophical format even in the modern teachings of the cultural traditions from which they originated.

In Europe, another spiritual system based on mediumship had gained popularity. Allen Kardec's Spiritism is in some ways similar to Spiritualism, but involves a fair number of differences. Most obviously, perhaps, is the difference in the idea of what constitutes spirits and what spirits can be contacted. Whereas Spiritualists are mainly interested in contacting the spirits of the deceased, Spiritists claim all spirits are of either a positive or negative sort, but many exist which are not deceased human beings at all. Additionally, Spiritism puts an emphasis on having everyone develop mediumistic skills, rather than focusing on a handful of gifted mediums.

Ultimately, Spiritualism lost popularity as an increase in pressure on mediums to give a good performance brought the focus off of spirit communication (which is, to be fair, usually quite boring) and onto the manifestation of physical results, which in turn forced even possibly legitimate mediums to commit fraud in order to guarantee customers. The uncovering of physical mediums as frauds brought a great deal of criticism on the Spiritualist movement.

At the same time, the Theosophical Society, which had never been a particularly large movement to begin with, but always a focus primarily of esotericists, also began to wane in popularity. This was in no small part due to Jiddu Krishnamurti renouncing the much-hyped title of "world teacher," which had been long promised by Annie Besant and C.W. Leadbeater. It did not do well through the tumult of the two world wars, but never fully vanished.[5] Instead, teachings about ascended masters were superceded by Aleister Crowley's Thelema in the popular magic of the time, or later merged into the various UFO cults of the 50s and 60s[6]. The New Age movement served as, if not a direct successor, at least a spiritual one.

With the New Age movement, the currency of the esoteric gained some traction again. Now with a greater exposure to information from other traditions, once again people sought to find what they were missing, approaching the occult with a renewed interest. Psychicism, magic, and so on were all back in vogue. As it popularized, however, the spirituality was not always well preserved, and people became more interested in the affectations than the effect. Along with the US military taking an interest at this time in psychic abilities,[7] the shift from spiritual to practical reflected the spirit of the time.

_____

[5] Indeed, the Theosophical Society still exists today and is quite healthy, as these things go.

[6] Many of the tenets of modern New Age UFO religions were established by Guy Ballard's "I AM" Activity in the 1930s, and carried forward from there.

[7] Projects CENTER LANE, STARGATE, GRILL FLAME, and others investigated psychic phenomena, primarily with a focus on

While parapsychology had always had an interest in the scientific investigation of psychic phenomena, these investigations historically did not attend to untestable notions of psychic energy, but instead focused on observable phenomena like telepathy or psychokinesis. Subtle energy manipulation was now no longer a side effect to spiritual attainment but an ability to be sought after on its own, or as a mechanism by which one could develop the more concrete abilities.

Parapsychology itself has contributed significantly to research on the paranormal in general, however. The parapsychological approach is a scientific approach based in empiricism and separate from spiritual claims. While there once was considerable overlap between dominant religious movements like Spiritualism and parapsychological research, this link was severed as parapsychology moved on. With a focus only on observable anomalous phenomena, parapsychology generally focuses its efforts only on observable effects that can be statistically measured. Remote viewing, telepathy via ganzfeld experiments[8], micro and macro PK[9], and other psychic feats can be tested. However, because subtle energy cannot be detected using any presently existing measuring tools, does not at this time have much to tell us about subtle energy itself.

---

remote viewing and psychokinesis, and in response to Russian and Chinese research into the same. Much of this research has been made available through the Freedom of Information Act and is available on the CIA website.

[8] A type of experiment using limited sensory stimulation, generally in the form of soft pink light over the eyes and white noise, which has proved beneficial in telepathy experiments. Notably advanced by Charles Honorton and Sharon Harper in 1974.

[9] While macro-PK experiments and effects remain difficult to demonstrate in laboratory conditions, the Princeton Engineering Anomalies Research (PEAR) Lab once conducted many micro-PK experiments and demonstrated effects fairly reliably.

A Philosophical Introduction to Subtle Energy

What, then, is this subtle energy? It is in essence a vaguely defined force or energy which seems to be directed by mental will and which can be used to affect material reality. The term "energy" is used only by convention – it is not energy in the sense used in physics, a property by which matter is heated or performs work. It cannot to date be measured technologically, and so for this reason it is better to use the spiritual model, rather than the materialist scientific model, to work with it.

This energy can be employed for a variety of reasons, including communication with others, protecting oneself from the psychic impressions of the environment, reproducing magical effects, or interacting with the physical environment or with living things. Direct energy manipulation is also frequently employed in the astral planes, where it seems much more effective generally. The uses of subtle energy in its direct form are myriad because it is, in essence, a method of directing will and a mechanism by which that will can take form. Adherents of this kind of magical work tend to focus on very direct and immediate results, with increased complexity taking increased work and generally branching into other fields at that point. Chaos magicians often find themselves quite comfortable with this kind of work, while ceremonial magicians often deride the practices as ineffective or inferior in their possible results. Generally, however, the goal of the ritualist is not the same as the goal of the energy worker. If a solitary difference had to be pointed out, it might be that the ritualist performs the rituals such that some external force brings about the result, while the energy worker aims to do the work him or herself. By doing so, the energy worker may have more immediate control or agency in the work, but also likely has significantly less power to bring it about.

Subtle energy manipulation is generally first learned by developing skill in visualization and meditation. Meditation can help calm our minds and the distractions that come from the conventional senses, making one more sensitive to the subtle movements of energy within and around the body. This meditation does not need to be strict or formal at first, but a strong meditative practice makes for an easier time going forward, in addition to being beneficial just generally in one's life. The skill of visualization goes together with meditation. Visualization is distinct from imagination because visualization is intended to be efficacious. That is, we visualize a result we actually intend to create by way of the visualization. Imagining something moving and visualizing something moving are different actions because the visualization is an intended or desired outcome. Consider an archer with a bow and arrow, taking aim at a target. Anyone can imagine twanging a bow and the arrow hitting the target, but when the archer *visualizes* the arrow hitting the target, he or she puts into motion the events to see it happen. The visualization directs the body what to do, and the body then does it. Similarly, by visualizing the movement of energy, we do not simply imagine it there, but rather intend it and so direct it.

Similarly, when we visualize a ball of energy forming, or visualize energy flowing to or from something, we are not pretending this is happening, but rather the act of visualization and the intent for it to be happening does in fact put the energy in motion. With greater levels of mental concentration and clearer, undistracted visualization we are able to move this energy with greater precision and strength, and so it becomes more effective. To this end, we find ourselves back at meditation, where the ability to still the mind until distracting thoughts are reduced benefits our concentration and so the effectiveness of our work.

The way that subtle energy is believed to work, where it originates, what its properties are, and so on are tied heavily to cultural traditions that recognize it and work with it, and so can be learned in much greater detail through the lens of a tradition that supports it. There is no single traditional understanding which transcends all cultural practices which have acknowledged it, though there are variations on themes. Because it defies the materialistic investigation of modern science, it cannot be described definitively outside the traditions in which its practice has been developed.

Ultimately, it is not so important what its objective scientific properties are – if it even has any at all – but rather what its subjective, experiential qualities are. Because it is directed by mind, because it affects mind and is affected by mind, it is more important that our understanding of subtle energy be *internally* consistent, rather than externally correspondent to some kind of dogma. I will attempt here to describe the framework and model of subtle energy work that works for me. I make no attempt to declare it the only truth or some absolute truth, but rather it is the model by which I have come to understand this subtle energy through my experience and study. While I believe this model is strong and leads to good results in working with energy, I do not mean to promote it as the only model, or even the best model for you. Still, I think it's a good enough framework to enable instruction and inquiry without discouraging learning.

The world, this phenomenal reality we all share, can be conceived of as divisible into three spheres or domains, existing in relation to one another without being entirely distinct or entirely separate.[10] These three spheres, planes, or realms can be graded in rank from coarse to subtle: the material or physical

---

[10] See Appendix B, on Hermetic Philosophy, for an esoteric philosophy which employs this model and from which much of the model presented in this book is extrapolated. It is not the only or first system to use this model, but it is one of the more prominent.

plane, the astral or energetic plane, and the mental or spiritual plane.

The material plane needs very little explanation as it is the physical world in which we all reside. It is the realm of books, tables, chairs, and people with physical, fleshy bodies. It is very coarse because it is conditioned by its own material nature. Because it is so coarse, it is easy to interact with through actually physical means, and much more difficult to interact with through subtle means. Bang two rocks together and you get an immediate result; run water over a rock and you still get a result, but it takes much longer. If you want to use the water to interact with the rock in the same way as you did when you banged two rocks together, that's going to take some know-how. The use of subtle energy in the physical world is like this too; a skilled use can bring about some kind of an effect, but it may just as well be better to use a physical tool.

The astral plane or energetic world is subtler, but not entirely subtle. It is a kind of consensus reality of minds. The astral reflects the world sometimes, but it is hazy, like a density in disturbed water. Powerful objects in the physical world reflect through, but objects of less consequence do not. The astral plane is additionally the domain of many spirits, who may have difficulty communicating in the physical world but can do so easily there. The astral does not correspond with the physical world in a one to one way, and because it is subtler it is much more easily influenced by our minds. Whereas in the material world it is difficult for our minds to manifest dramatic results, in the astral this is not so difficult at all. Astral projection has long been a practice of ceremonial magicians and energy workers alike, as both are able to more easily communicate with and interact with spirits there, as well as to work spells and manifest the results they wish to see reflected down on the material plane.

The mental plane is the most fickle and pernicious and is subtler still. Here, our ability to concentrate is very important as the mental plane's subtlety allows it to be affected by mere thought. It is in essence an abstraction of our own minds, and as fickle and subject to change as our thoughts are from moment to moment. Here is the place of ideas and concepts that we hold, not held together strongly by consensus but rather subject to whimsy and distraction. We also interact with the mental plane through perception of the astral and the physical planes. The act of perception is a mental one; whereas sensation occurs through a physical process and a sensory organ, perception is a process of cognition. What we sense with our eyes, for example, provides mental information which we process, coming up with what we think or feel about a thing. In a constant loop of cognition, we gain new information and, based on that information, we change our opinions or apply them to the objects we are sensing. This overlay, originating from our own minds, is the substance of the mental plane.

Indeed, the three planes described here are in truth not entirely distinct one from another but instead are mutually interdependent, one upon another. It is through this non-distinction that the manipulation of subtle energy works at all. The mental plane of thought projects down through the astral and affects our perceptions of both the astral and the physical, while the physical in turn affects the mental plane through sensation and these both are reflected in the astral. The manipulation of the subtle energy on the astral can bring about effects in the physical, and changes we make in the material world similarly reflect through to the astral. By focusing our will in the mental plane this can manifest astrally as well as physically, and so we come back around to the importance of meditation as the direction of this subtle energy is facilitated by strong and acutely focused will.

Again, this is certainly not the only model describing the manipulation of subtle energy. It lacks nuance, but it effectively addresses three domains that will be important going forward. Other systems of magic and mysticism will divide these planes differently, sometimes in great nuance and detail and other times less so. Some will substitute others, and these systems are themselves likely valid and functional. I do in fact encourage studying them as having a more robust theoretical model can inform not only the development of subtle energy abilities but the more important spiritual development. The model provided here can be considered less a dogmatic assertion of reality-as-it-is, and more an abstraction or model that can be used conceptually for the manipulation of energy. Though superficially similar to Hermetic or Rosicrucian ideas,[11] it neglects the aspects of the divine,[12] as the direct subtle energy manipulation and psychic practices in this book are not dependent on them. I have, however, also made an attempt to prevent this model from clashing with other, more robust models, so as to facilitate the learning of the practitioner already adherent to one or many philosophical models of magic.[13]

By understanding this model we can get an idea of how working with this subtle energy actually goes about affecting change, physically or astrally. While again this is merely a conceptual model for how these things work, it does help with

---

[11] Rosicrucianism is a religious philosophy largely derived from Hermeticism, as well as Qabbalah and esoteric Christianity.

[12] Many magical traditions based on Hermeticism, such as Rosicrucianism, the Golden Dawn, or so on, ascribe properties of divinity to the various planes, through relation to the Qabbalistic Tree of Life or in other ways.

[13] In the writing of this book I have made deliberate efforts to ensure that the practice of subtle energy manipulation as presented will not directly interfere with a student who is already an adept in another system. With that in mind, adepts of more complete magical systems should defer to their own traditions when there is a clash. This work stands on its own for the reader who desires only to develop psychic abilities or manipulate subtle energy as an end to itself, but is insufficient for the mystical practices of the magus or yogi.

both conceiving of and visualizing the processes involved. It is important too, however, to not let it get in the way of very practical exercises while trying to overthink. I have provided this framework more as a method by which more advanced students can benefit and conceive of what they are doing than as a bit of dogma to be memorized or adhered to for these exercises to work.

However we choose to conceive of the methods by which subtle energy manipulation works, the practical effective element is this visualization or focused *intent* by which we direct the energy in various pursuits. Whether we are simply massing energy up or moving it around, making shapes or elaborate constructs, imprinting objects or removing those imprints, the basic mechanic of moving energy about remains roughly the same. Focusing first on feeling the energy out, and then directing our attention so that the energy follows this, either unimpeded through space or along natural channels, we can direct this subtle energy however we choose.

As for the source of subtle energy, the framework provided also gives us some insight. Firstly, it explains or at least acknowledges the energetic body, a kind of subtle energetic component or echo of the physical body which generally occupies the same area in space both physically and astrally, but which is capable of moving about independent of the physical body in both the astral and material worlds. Because this astral or energetic body is related to our physical bodies, harm to the energetic body will over time harm the physical body and vice versa. Similarly, it is entirely possible to affect, draw energy from, or manipulate energy of other people's energetic bodies. Energy does not "belong" to a specific person and so we can draw this energy from effectively any source.

The *quality* of the energy can be considered using the classical alchemical elements. The source of the energy, or what the energy is associated with in the material plane, will determine its elemental composition; if it's mostly fire, or water, or earth, or air, and in what proportions. Most things are comprised in part of all of the different elements. This is especially true of living organisms, where the various elements rule different biological functions. This too remains largely unimportant at the basic level and will only really come into play when working with more advanced magical functions or substituting for spells and suchlike. The energy *itself* is naturally rather generic, taking on qualities as it is worked with, and the elemental qualities of energy can be ignored when drawing it, or removed later. It seems as if this subtle energy is naturally without qualities, but that exposure to objects and elements and so on, astrally or physically, imparts or imprints those qualities onto it. This process of imprinting is natural to energy, and often associated with objects being "cursed" or "haunted" or creating an experience of certain feeling or emotions.

For the purpose of working with subtle energy in the most generic sense, it is possible to simply draw generic "energy" from most sources, and this energy needs not be programmed or deprogrammed. This generic energy is what most subtle energy workers prefer to work with in the last few years, and it avoids problems with elemental work that come from inexperience. More on elemental work will be discussed as we get to the chapter on spellcasting.

In the end, the qualities of subtle energy can be known, but not its actual substance. Some speculation includes that subtle energy is consciousness itself, interacting with the physical world. After all, we direct energy with consciousness. We imprint energy and give it qualities with consciousness. Through energy, we can access the ways in which others have also imprinted objects through interacting with them. All people program and imprint energy through their interaction with mundane physical objects. It is the interaction of their consciousness, of their mind, with the physical world that imbues qualities on objects which can be detected by others through psychometry.

Whether energy is an extension of consciousness, something that interacts with consciousness, or a model of working with consciousness itself cannot be determined except through experience. But, if this is the case, it is not "energy" at all. This may be so! This "energy" is a model, something for our mind to interact with. Much like chakras or energy channels, it is a conceptual tool to allow our limited minds to make sense of an experience that defies our conventional senses. We should not get too stuck on the idea of energy as having properties of its own. Instead, we can work with it using a model that works for us to organize information, without becoming too fixed on the idea that this is "how it really is."

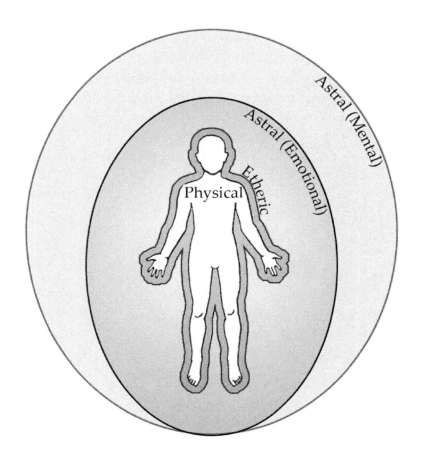

Figure 1- The Energy Body

THE ENERGY BODY

There are as many descriptions of the anatomy of the energy body as there are practitioners of subtle energy systems. By far the most prominent today comes to us by way of the Theosophical Society. This model includes the chakras, which have already been discussed as not being true anatomical structures within the body, but symbolic intersections. The model I prefer is based on later theosophical models, more from Annie Besant and Rudolf Steiner, less from Blavatsky and Leadbeater.

The energy body generally refers to those parts of our body that don't exist in the physical. We shouldn't consider that we have a separate physical body and energetic body. Instead, it is better to think of ourselves as having a body, and that body is comprised of many parts. Some of those parts are the physical parts we see, and some are more subtle.

We can arbitrarily divide this unified vision of the body into parts, however. Of course, we are already familiar with the physical body, as this is the coarsest aspect that exists in the material plane. Slightly more subtle than this is the *etheric body*. Then even more subtle still is the *astral body*, which we can divide into the lower and higher, or near and far, astral. The rough organization of these bodies is pictured in Figure 1 on page 24.

The etheric body is the energetic body that corresponds to the physical body. Just as physical objects have energetic fields around them onto and from which we can imprint and read information, our physical body also has a subtle energy field. There is a subtle energy heart, subtle lungs, subtle ribs, and so on. These correspond closely to the physical, and they directly interact. When healers claim to be able to tell illness based on the vibrancy of the energy body, this is what they are referring to. A dull and diminished etheric stomach may indicate a full stomach, while a dull and diminished etheric lung indicates congestion. These are impressions that take considerable skill to be able to read accurately, of course.

What is important to recognize is that the etheric body corresponds closely to the physical body. Its outermost bounds are usually about three to six inches from the surface of the skin. The root chakra is its symbolic intersection with the physical body. It is the grounding root or tether that connects these two. Instability in this chakra tends to bring with it physical distress. More information on the Chakras is found in Appendix A.

It is also important to recognize that the correspondence between the physical and etheric bodies is not a one-way street. The health and status of the physical body is reflected in the etheric body. Because of this, the etheric body is more difficult to influence by psychic means. We must overcome the stabilizing influence of the material body. At the same time, however, influences on the etheric body *do* affect the physical body. Successfully impressing information onto the etheric body will bring about slow but certain changes in the physical body. Sometimes, these can be abrupt and dramatic effects. Usually, however, they are far more insipid. It is very important that we take care to ensure our etheric body's health and to not strain our etheric body too much, lest those effects be manifested in the physical body.

Next, beyond the etheric form, is the near astral body. This is what anthroposophist Rudolf Steiner described as the emotional body. It is astral in nature, overlapping the physical body and the astral body. This body reflects our emotions, and is deeply connected to our emotional state. It expands and contracts based on our emotions. Happy, positive states expand this body and cause it to vibrate or radiate brighter, while depressive states tend to restrict it and make it duller. This body usually extends approximately 3 feet from the physical body in all directions. It is what most people refer to when talking about the *aura*.

Like the etheric body, it is responsive to the physical body and similarly affects the physical body. When we are happy, this field reflects that. When we are psychically attacked or exposed to negative energies in the environment, this field also interacts with those fields and our emotions adjust accordingly. Some people are far more sensitive to this kind of emotional information from their environments, and we call those people *empaths*. This is not the only way empathy can function, but it is a common way. All energetic sensation is based on the interactions of our energy fields with the energy fields of the worlds around us. Each of us has our own dispositions and sensitivities, just as we each have our own sensitivity of taste or smell or sight.

When we are in an environment that is oppressively charged with patterned energies, either intentionally or through some unconscious process, our energy field will reflect this. Based on our own sensitivity, our mood and physical state will change as well. The emotional body is symbolically connected to the physical and etheric bodies through the sacral and heart chakras.

Beyond the near astral is the far or higher astral, what Steiner would refer to as the thought body. This is the least dense form of the body. Like the emotional body, it encompasses all of the previous bodies. It also expands and contracts based on our awareness. Because of its non-spatial characteristics, existing in the astral, it can be said that anything that enters our awareness exists within the astral body. If something comes into our consciousness, this is reflected in our astral body. So, the astral body usually encompasses our immediate environment, extending between 12 and 25 feet from the physical body. For accomplished meditators and powerful yogis, it can extend far beyond that, based on their awareness.

When we think about far away locations, those locations are reflected in our astral body, and vice versa, even though there is no physical connection. This is because the astral body exists outside of conventional space, more in the mental planes.

Just as emotions are embodied in the emotional astral body, thoughts and perceptions are embodied in the mental astral body. Similarly, interactions between the astral body and the environment can lead to imprinting. Mostly this comes into play when we are in contact with other conscious beings, as the astral bodies will exchange and synchronize over time. For our purposes, telepathy can be understood as the interaction between astral bodies in the mental plane leading to the arising of thoughts (in a pre-conceptual, seed form) within our minds. The energetic environment around us can also affect our thoughts, and this is a way in which spirits can communicate with us. As our astral bodies overlap theirs, they are able to impress ideas onto us, and so we can impress ideas onto them as well.

The intersection of the astral and etheric bodies is the third eye chakra, which governs perception. When these chakras are unified into an expanded state, and we enter states of *Samadhi*, or higher meditative states of awareness, this is usually referred to as the activation of the crown chakra.

All of these bodies are unified, however. They are aggregated into a whole that we call "self." Rudolf Steiner considered this a fourth body, which he called the ego-self. He then further delineated other subtle bodies corresponding to spiritual concepts. The traditional theosophical model also includes a fifth layer called the spiritual body. Because they are not relevant to psychic functioning or the manipulation or sensation of subtle energy, they have been omitted here. The spiritual body in particular is related entirely to theosophical conceptions of the world, and Steiner's egoic body relates to his own model of spiritual progression.

RELIGION AND SPIRITUALITY

The silver lining, the flipside to the lack of a spiritual or religious model that informs or guides energetic practice, is that the direct manipulation of subtle energy requires no adherence or commitment to a spiritual or religious path. While this lack of commitment can present a handicap to a system of magic, it does make the practice of energy working *itself* something that can be practiced by someone of any religious tradition or spiritual path, or none at all. Historically various religions have issued prohibitions against magical working, "witchcraft," or so on.[14] These prohibitions are often because the use of magical powers, as it is understood by the people of the time, depended on demons or other deities from other religions to perform. When working directly with the subtle energy, this is not a concern. The energy worker is responsible for his or her own actions, and is the sole source of the power and capability being used. There is no need to dedicate oneself to a new path, or to forsake a path one is already on.

Religious or cultural prohibitions can particularly be a concern for children who demonstrate a natural aptitude for either energy working or general psychic abilities. It is not unheard of for a child who demonstrates such paranormal feats as telepathy, clairvoyance, or psychokinesis to be denounced as possessed by a demon, for example. This unfortunately often leads to persecution from the community and to unhappy consequences for the child. Needless to say, it is far better to cultivate these preternatural abilities than to suppress them, and

---

[14] This dates back at least as far as the biblical story of King Saul, who was punished for consulting with the Witch of Endor in 1 Samuel 38. We don't need to look that far however, as we can look at modern proscriptions against it in for example Saudi Arabia and Iran, or various Blue Laws prohibiting it in places throughout the United States, and so on.

especially to suppress them in the name of religion. Here I use the term preternatural very carefully, as it is distinct from the supernatural. While supernatural results come from higher forces than nature, preternatural abilities are those which, while uncommon and unexplained, derive not from gods or demons but from the wielder him or herself. A subtle energy manipulator does not rely on any higher power for their abilities, and in the case of young children experiencing these things they often did not seek out this kind of thing at all in the first place.

It's also certainly not true that this is the only way these things work, or that any psychic ability one demonstrates must come from this kind of neutral source. Other magical traditions which work with deities or spirits or which work with energy in a different way can all be magically efficacious. While the results should be noticeable by the subtle energy worker, it will not necessarily be comprehensible or sensible due to the way it is worked. Put another way, magical systems using their own traditions take on a flavor of that tradition that the subtle energy worker may be able to detect but not describe or emulate. Direct manipulation of subtle energy isn't the only game in town, and it isn't the secret way in which all the other systems *actually* work but for their obscuration of dogma. Instead, this is a system that has been built over time by syncretism and poaching working bits from other systems until eventually it came into its own (mostly) coherent whole. As I mentioned before, when a more robust system presents itself, if one is so inclined, it is often better to follow that.

Subtle energy work *can* however serve as a supplement to those that do work with other energies. While the Christian can rest assured that they will not be working with demons or so on if working exclusively with this energy, the pagan can just as easily rest assured that they will not interfere with their own magical working through practicing with subtle energy, and they may in fact find it fruitful to augment their spells.

It is also commonly misunderstood that children with psychic "gifts" are somehow advantaged, and that only people with these kinds of gifts can develop any kind of psychic aptitude. Both of these are largely incorrect. To the first point, oftentimes children with innate aptitude for psychic abilities tend to be marginalized, and identified as mentally ill or emotionally unstable, or in some cases possessed or haunted by demons, and so on. Such labeling and mistreatment only compounds the confusion and difficulty that can arise from having senses or experiences without others to observe dealing with the same experiences to learn from. Children who are raised by parents with similar abilities tend not to fare poorly, but much of what we learn as children comes from observation and interaction with adults with the same experiences and circumstances, and for the psychic child with parents who do not model this experience, or who actively disbelieve in and suppress it, it can be very difficult. These children do not learn methods of control or inhibition of their psychic senses and so can end up developing mental illness anyhow.

It is perhaps more harmful to believe that one's own experiences cannot be trusted than it is to have untrustworthy experiences. The telepathic child who knows what others are thinking, even if just on a subconscious level, quickly finds him or herself in trouble for calling people out, or acting too directly on people's thoughts, which can be unsettling for the thinker. The empathic child who does not recognize the source of emotions as being outside him or herself and so struggles to find emotional calm can be difficult to soothe or manage, and ultimately may end up harmed. The child who can sense spirits and is told that these spirits aren't real, just part of the imagination, but whose experiences don't stop them from having these experiences will doubt his or her own sanity. All of this is stems from misunderstanding and mistreatment of these conditions in children, and all of this can be prevented by identifying these conditions as what they really are and teaching children accordingly. Still, the tendency for these children to end up suffering even into adulthood certainly calls into question the idea of these abilities as "gifts."

For these reason we must take care not to wrap our work with subtle energy up with too much religious or spiritual context except where our own spiritual systems demand it. Numerous religions and spiritual paths define this energy differently, and ascribe different characteristics to it. The somewhat sterilized language employed here does not quite do justice to the concept in any one school of thought, but does enough to demonstrate how it can be employed in ways similar to those in religious traditions or so on. When working specifically with subtle energy, our own concepts about how it "should" behave, coming from our own cultural contexts, will to some extent limit how we work. This energy, after all, is responsive to thought and intent. If we do not believe that a particular approach is possible, or that energy can behave in a certain way, or accomplish certain tasks, we will not succeed as we will not be able to formulate our intent. We must move past our own concepts of how things work in order to see how they actually can work.

When this occurs, or when something clashes with a belief system, we should try it anyhow and, if it works, rather than discarding one or the other we can simply identify that it is "something else." After all, none of this is concrete, and so there is no good reason to believe that all subtle energy work employs the *same* subtle energy. We must not fall into the trap of making an extreme stretch of syncretism and saying that, for example, the Soviet concept of bioplasma or the American concept of psychoenergy is exactly the same as the Tibetan *lung* or Japanese *ki*. So, the common sense answer when this subtle energy behaves in a way that we do not believe to be possible because of our religious ideas is to acknowledge that perhaps some other mechanism is in play, without trying too hard to put specific labels on it. Whether something is *ki* or *prana* or *bioplasma* is irrelevant, we can conventionally label it based on how it behaves, but with no concrete significant to point to, the signifier becomes academic.

It should also be noted that it is not uncommon for the subtle energy manipulator to sometimes encounter spirits of religious significance or claiming to have religious significance, especially when they begin practicing things covered in the latter half of this book, such as astral projection. For this reason it is somewhat necessary to maintain an open mind. That maybe should go without saying in a book discussing the magical employment of invisible energies, but religious dogmatism can cause people to believe strange things.

I advise caution when engaging with spirits of purportedly religious significance that you encounter during any kind of magical work, including astral projection. It is especially worthy of a degree of skepticism when such spirits engage or interact with us through channels atypical of their religious type. Many religions and spiritual paths have established channels through which spirits communicate messages, such as prophecy or prophets that take understood forms, or through evocation or invocation, or whatever else. If a spirit is contacting us purporting to be of one religion, and turning out to be another, then this is suspicious and rates skepticism. Similarly, a spirit that tells us things contrary to what we know or understand of a religious belief system should be viewed with skepticism. These are two easy and simple tests the violation of which may indicate that we should dismiss the spirit entirely, at the very least as not being what it is representing itself as.

For similar reasons, it becomes important to be familiar with how spirits might manifest, or what they tend to appear as, so that we can recognize things when we do encounter them. Such encounters with incorporeal spirits are never clear, but we do ourselves no favors by being utterly unfamiliar with them.

SELF-CARE

Despite that subtle energy does not seem to be any form of physical matter or wave and does not seem to be subject to the understood rules of physics or so on, it turns out that a person can become physically exhausted through working with subtle energy. Nina Kulagina, the renowned Soviet psychokinetic, reported pain in her spine and would appear to physically exert herself while working, and this is consistent with the experience of other psychokinetics I've met. The manipulation of subtle energy, while not necessarily the same as psychokinesis, can also lead to physical exhaustion, muscle pain, mental exhaustion, and so on. It is important to take care not to allow oneself to overexert or overwork, as injury can create greater setbacks than any kind of delay in practice would cause. Many beginning energy workers have a tendency to over-exert due to a combination of enthusiasm and the mistaken idea that manipulating subtle energy could not have physical or mental consequences for them.

Throughout the book good energetic hygiene and health practices will be discussed, but it is also important to take care of our physical bodies when working with energy. If physical effects of energetic overexertion, commonly things like twitching, restlessness, muscle pain or soreness, headache, disorientation, or so on appear, it is important to try eating something, ideally something with sugar and potassium. The link between sugar and potassium and subtle energy work is poorly understood but may have to do with the kind of neurological effort involved. Orange juice, bananas, peanuts, or even chocolate milk are good "recovery foods" when working with psychic phenomena of any type. If these kinds of physical symptoms are experienced, it's important also to take a break. Pushing too far can lead to, for example, seizures or collapse. While this is somewhat uncommon, it is not unheard of, and certainly not worth risking versus simply taking a break to do something else for a while when one begins to feel fatigued.

Energetic fatigue often mirrors symptoms of physical fatigue, including minor aches and pains, sharp pains, confusion, loss of mental acuity, and so on. It is important before and after performing any of the exercises in this book to maintain an honest and mindful assessment of how one feels, both physically and emotionally. While subtle energy work can itself be physically exhausting, other practices detailed in this book, such as telepathy and empathy, or clairvoyance, or astral projection, can have their own emotional or physical impacts.

Empathy in particular can bring us into contact with emotions which we may not be prepared to handle. For many of us, the emotional and psychological load of encountering, for example, a suicidal person, or someone going through tremendous sufferings, may be shocking and disturbing. A person who has never contacted another's thoughts may have difficulty understanding the things that run through the minds of others. And of course anyone who seeks to look at hidden things must be prepared for what he or she may see. Thus, self-care should not be considered simply as taking a rest when one feels tired, and should also be extended to include mindfulness of our own mental state as well. Maintaining self-awareness of our mental state is the key to ensuring that when it is being affected by psychic contact with the emotions of others, we do not mistake this for our own emotional state and act on it.

Taking stock of how we feel prior to beginning work therefore becomes a critical part of our psychic preparation. It also sets a better baseline against which to compare empathic or telepathic information we come into contact with, and, as we will soon learn, also allows us to better sense the imprinted energy with which we come into contact through our day.

LEARNING PSYCHIC ENERGY WORK

Everyone possesses the faculties for learning subtle energy manipulation and the capacity for intuition, telepathy, empathy, clairvoyance, and so on. Many of these skills can be mediated through the energy body itself, something we all have. Though the exact mechanisms by which these abilities are possible is not known to science, the framework presented here works. Energy itself does not seem to be the actual force behind many demonstrations of telepathy, empathy, and clairvoyance, but it does work for those purposes.

The development of those faculties without an energetic framework is likely to occur if someone follows deeply down the path of meditation alone. These skills were once called *siddhis*, or attainments, and are the fruits of meditative accomplishment. This path can take many years, however, and relies on a spiritual path and spiritual guidance that I cannot provide. For some people, developing telepathy, empathy, and the like will happen automatically as they learn to pay attention and note their environments and surroundings. For others, it will not be obvious at all. We are all unique and different.

Additionally, because our energetic bodies are similarly unique, the sensations and impressions we get from energy change. Internal consistency will be the most important factor in learning psychic ability.

Above all, mindset is critical to developing psychic ability. The single greatest factor contributing to the demonstration of psychic phenomena is cultural acceptability. In cultures that are "psi positive," which accept the paranormal as normal and which recognize psychic abilities as things everyone has, psi phenomena are demonstrated far more easily. In cultures that do not hold belief in the paranormal, it is much more difficult.

Our mindset, and our recognition that these abilities are normal and common to everyone, is critical to our ability to learn. This does not mean a blind belief or accepting these things on faith. We should absolutely test these things for ourselves. By cultivating the receptive faculty, however, it is very common that we should be able to plainly observe psychic ability in our own lives.

If at any time things are not working, remind yourself that you are already psychic. Like any skill, psychic ability takes practice. I often relate it to other senses: we all have our own psychic aptitude as a base, but with practice and training we can improve on it. The sommelier may have the natural ability to discern tastes, but without training, he or she cannot identify wines readily at all. And it is entirely possible that a person without "supertasting" will, with training, far surpass the untrained supertaster.

Caroline Dweck identified that one of the greatest factors in our success in any skill is our mindset. Those who believe that skill is fixed and distributed naturally, and that practice cannot lead to significant growth, avoid anything that doesn't come naturally to them. Those who recognize that skills can be learned and developed through dedication and practice, who have a growth mindset, can accomplish their goals.

We must strive to have a growth mindset, to practice, and to set realistic expectations. When I was young, I was told I am a natural psychic. I believed it then, and as a result I never learned to suppress or ignore my intuition and psychic senses. But the truth is, everyone is a natural psychic. The challenge is not in learning to do something we cannot do, but in learning to improve at a skill. Psychic ability development is skill development. Subtle energy work is no different from learning to play an instrument or a sport or to do a job. If you apply yourself, you can succeed.

MEDITATION AND OBSERVATION

Starting out with basic energy work does take a bit of preparation to begin. As mentioned before, a basic practice of meditation and strength of visualization will assist with this. Meditation in this sense does not need to be the rigorous meditation we see in Zen centers, complete with posture correcting beatings. Instead, it is best to sit comfortably in a chair ideally without a headrest so as to keep the head up under one's own power, but however one is most comfortable. Resting like this, allow the mind to rest on a single object or process and simply point the mind here. Common examples include counting of breaths, resting the mind on a small object such as a pebble, or even a small candle light. This meditative practice serves purely to allow the mind to rest and is not an attempt to think of anything in particular.

As we sit and rest the mind on, for example, the breath, we will find that the mind quite naturally will wander away. We'll find ourselves thinking about any number of things: whether we're meditating right, how good we're doing at the meditation, how much time is left before we can move on. The mind does not like to relax and instead will travel all over the place finding things to think about that are not the simple awareness of being in a place. This does not constitute a failure of meditation, but rather a recognition of how our minds tend to be. When we inevitably catch our mind having wandered off to wherever it has gone, we should do nothing with this but reset our attention on our breath. If we find ourselves returning again and again to the same thoughts, we should acknowledge that this is something we are concerned about, and return to the breath. It is not necessary, and in fact sometimes distractingly difficult, to cut the thoughts off, but it is important that we develop the skill of recognizing when the mind has wandered and returning it to the task at hand.

It is important not to rely too heavily on crutches for this kind of focus. Music does not assist us with focusing but rather distracts us in such a way as to allow our mind to spend its "extra cycles" attending to the music. Rather than helping us stay focused, it helps us stay distracted. This can be easily seen by observing that we can have songs "stuck in our head," which represent both our mind's attempt to fill in things that are not there, as well as the habituation of our mind to certain stimuli.

We should also avoid the misconceived notion that we are attempting to achieve a state without any kind of thinking at all. The organ of the brain performs certain functions and thought is one of them. We are not attempting to silence the mind and attain thoughtlessness; that is sometimes the goal of various religious meditations or practices but in this case we instead simply want to gain a recognition of the nature of our mind, what it does when we leave it alone; and, by doing so, we want to habituate it to resting rather than wandering. Again considering the notion of hearing music long after we've left the concert, our minds are strongly conditioned and patterned by what we subject them to and how we use them. By practicing just sitting every so often – daily, if possible – we can habituate the mind towards relaxedness that is conducive to focus not just for the purpose of energy working but in fact just for general wellbeing.

Having done this, we will find that after a few sessions of practice our mind wanders less and less, instead staying focused on our focal point for longer and longer periods of time uninterrupted. There is no benchmark or requirement for time that we can focus, but in this case the longer we can concentrate on having set our mind on a task, the better. More importantly, we've taught the mind not to merely wander off, and we are teaching ourselves that this is undesirable. A focused mind is a more effective mind, especially when it comes to psychic or magical work.

Once we have gained some stability and comfort with this kind of focus, the mind will naturally be able to focus on new tasks with a greater precision. This habituation towards a resting mind allows us to maintain a kind of unworried focus that does not pattern energy unnecessarily with the various thoughts that arise and emotions of concern, worry, and rushedness that often accompany 21st century living. Instead, the calm, collected, stable thoughts lead to calm, collected, stable energetic results. Just as a tempestuous storm might affect construction of a building, where peaceful, pleasant weather would make that same construction both easier and stronger, a calm steady mind leads to more effective energy working, and a disturbed, distracted mind leads to distracted energetic results. Energy being directly patterned by our thoughts, this should not come as any sort of surprise. Whatever emotions or mental conditions we bring to the work will be reflected in its results.

The ability to rest and quiet the mind therefore is a strong foundation for focused, clean energy work without undesired patterning, and which can be achieved much easier. Another method for assisting with this goal is *grounding*, through which we take already patterned energy surrounding us and dump it away. As energy around us is patterned and imprinted by our emotional states, distracted minds, and so on throughout the day it accumulates in our "field" and causes us some instability.

But this is not the only goal of meditation. In the end, we should strive to find estrangement in those thoughts. We should recognize that those thoughts are not "us" but rather an experience that happens to us. Stopping thinking would be like stopping the waves at the beach. The sounds of waves do not distract us, and we can remain focused without identifying with our thoughts. When we do this, we can begin to analyze our thoughts, feelings, and sensations. We can start to recognize which ones belong to us by some natural process, and which come to us through some kind of extrasensory channel. Without this kind of analysis, we will struggle to recognize intuition as intuition. Highly sensitive individuals may acknowledge that information and act on it in the form of "hunches" or "gut feelings," without further analysis. Others will ignore it entirely, despite it arising on its own. The meditator begins to see these things naturally, however. So our focus on meditation is not just an exercise in focus and attention. While that is a benefit, the much greater benefit comes from our ability to notice a wider array of information that does not come to us through the conventional senses to which we habitually pay attention.

The next stage, after calm-abiding, is turning the mind towards noticing our internal states wherever we go. We will have already begun noticing our internal states as they change and in different locations simply through the practice of calm abiding. Now, with a stable mind, we can focus on looking deliberately at what is going on inside our bodies that might *not* be the result of our normal environment. We will notice that wherever we are, there are subtle impressions made on our emotional state, on our thoughts, and even on our physical body.

Take notes about these different sensations as they arrive in different places, paying special attention to how they are felt in the body. Learn to identify the associations between bodily feelings, emotional states, ideas and habits of thoughts, and your surroundings. As you come to understand different places better, and particularly as you take notes of the feelings, you will come to appreciate the beginnings of sensing energy. Perhaps more importantly, by taking notes on how these things feel, you will develop a vocabulary for discussing energetic impressions.

Because each of us has a unique energy body, it is actually difficult to say what energy *feels like*. What my body may manifest as feelings of magnetism or pulsation, another person might feel as flowing water or as heat. The same thing is being sensed, but because of the unique properties of our energetic bodies and the way they interface with our physical bodies, the sensation is different. It is possible neither of us is sensing incorrectly. However, it's also possible one of us is. The only way we can be sure is through internal consistency. If I routinely feel a certain kind of energy as magnetism, then when I feel magnetism I can draw a connection.

Building a robust situational vocabulary allows us to bring nuance into our perception of the subtle world. It is common for therapists to teach their patients many new emotion words, as most people have a limited emotional vocabulary. With a limited emotional vocabulary, people cannot express what they are feeling with enough nuance to address the problem. The remedy for indignation is different than for fury, which is different still from frustration, or aggravation, or so on. All of these may just be called "anger" and we won't get anywhere. Similarly, if we do not develop vocabulary to differentiate feelings of energy, we will constantly end up describing everything the same way. The sensations may be subtly different, but because we have no words to work with, we are left describing it with little accuracy.

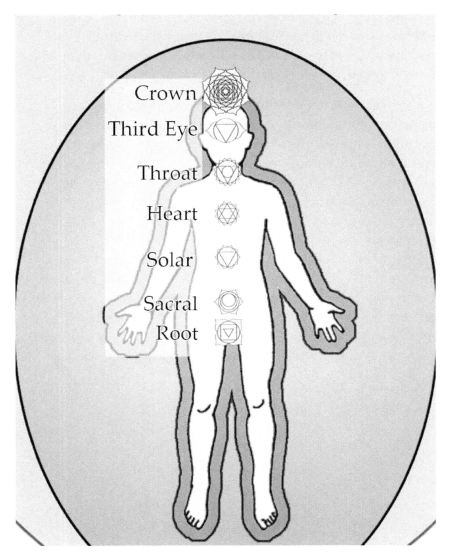

Figure 2 - The Chakras

DIRECTING ENERGY WITHIN THE BODY

The next basic foundational skill for the beginning subtle energy worker is the movement of energy within the body. Generally our bodies manage their own energetic health automatically, a result of the function of the body itself and its causes and conditions. Moving energy willfully about the body does not necessarily interrupt this process, just as holding one's breath doesn't interrupt the function of the entire body. Assuming temporary, conscious control over the movement of energy is generally non-harmful and serves as a useful exercise for developing visualization skills and a sense for energy. It also serves as the foundation for any kind of energy work where we control energy externally without projecting it out from ourselves. Much as a punch originates from the shoulder and not the hand, energy work where we reach with tendrils of energy, or even project energy, begin from where we are. It is possible to work with energy without these kinds of connections, but that is a more advanced application. In any case, the movement of energy within our own bodies and energetic fields is the next step towards developing a practice of subtle energy manipulation.

To do this, we should first start by entering into the meditative state, grounding, and centering. Having done this, rest and attend to the body, shifting attention from one part of the body to another. Resting, attend to our feelings at our feet, moving up the legs, attend to our feelings in the stomach, the chest, and out through the arms to the tips of the fingers. Just rest your attention on this, not trying to do anything, but just being aware of what that area feels like. Relax the body, noting any particular areas of tension, stress, pain, discomfort, and so on. We are just taking a baseline here, getting a sense of what the body feels like left on its own.

Now, maintaining this same resting awareness, choose a place to shift some energy, for example, your hand. Setting our awareness on the hand, as before where we centered and grounded, breathe in and focus on energy coming to the energetic center below the navel, and, breathing out, visualize this energy flowing naturally along channels to your hand, and pooling there. With each breath, repeat this, noting the sensations that arise. When visualizing the channels, do not struggle to make them complete or to correspond sharply like an anatomical diagram in some way. Those familiar with traditional Chinese medicine, acupuncture, or so on may already have a working knowledge of the energetic channels in those systems and it is certainly fine to use those energetic anatomies for these purposes, but it is not at all necessary to do so. The energy, as it is being directed, will naturally move along these channels as the channels are really nothing more than the paths energy naturally takes flowing through the body. Visualizing them is a method of directing the intention, the energy will move as directed whether we know with pinpoint accuracy the flow path or not.

There are a lot of potential physical sensations associated with the perception of energy. Most commonly are feelings of warmth, pressure, or pulsing. Sometimes people feel vibrating, coolness, or other sensations. It's also entirely possible to not have any kinds of physical sensations from the movement of energy, and so this result should not be discarded. Generally, however, you yourself are the best gauge of whether or not this exercise succeeds. As the visualization and sensory mappings improve, movement of this energy will become more responsive as will a sense of success or failure. If you have a partner, you can work with them, sending energy to various parts of your own body at first and letting them attempt to sense where that is. Without a partner, this can still be done practicing with experienced energy workers from a distance, or you can rely on your own senses. As with many skills, as your proficiency improves the amount of effort required to move energy will be reduced until it seems to respond automatically and without any real effort.

Having completed the exercise, remember to ground and center again. In this case, you should do it because you have moved energy around in ways not part of your normal energetic flow. While leaving it there is probably not harmful and it would dissipate over time, it is good to get in the habit of taking self-care when working with energy. By grounding and centering we flush out the energetic focuses and allow the body's natural field to restore itself.

The practical benefits of moving energy within the body are usually not immediately clear, and are presented here as an exercise that should first be practiced to gain control over subtle energy itself. It is not however utterly without uses. In a later chapter we will discuss healing, and healing oneself by moving energy within the body is very viable. However, it is generally better to do so only after one has studied and trained in one of a variety of energetic healing systems, and in any case this application is dependent on skills discussed later in this book.

This is an exercise that we should not neglect and move on from, however. The movement of energy within the body is something we can easily sense through physical feedback that lets us know when we are succeeding.

Visualization is the means by which we communicate our intention to the energetic field and in turn the way we manipulate subtle energy. However, the effect of visualization alone is very small, and we must build and train the association between visualization and the movement of energy. Revisiting this exercise can help build that association strongly.

Psychometry and Imprinting

Psychometry is the ability to read information on objects, essentially through sensing changes in the energy body. Through the meditation and "just noticing" exercises, we have already begun practicing psychometry. As mentioned before, the energy body itself is your body's "sensor" for energetic changes. As we interact with the world, our energetic field comes into contact with the energy fields of objects around us. These energy fields create an impression on our field. When we focus the mind on the sensations arising from our energy field, we can detect the subtle changes that come from these interactions.

All objects are imprinted upon through interaction with consciousnesses. Later in this chapter we will discuss how we can deliberately imprint objects with ideas, information, feelings, or so on. But in fact this process is also performed unconsciously, all the time. By learning to recognize these impressions on objects, we can learn to sense information about objects simply by interacting with them.

The process of psychometry is relatively straightforward if we have been diligent about practicing our meditation and noticing skills. However, some additional information can help with our senses. First, if we are primarily dealing with energy through physical sensation as through "just noticing," we ideally want physical contact with the object[15]. This places the object inside our etheric field. Because the object itself has an etheric field, these two fields interact well; and, because the etheric field is closely connected to the physical body, it can easily create physical sensations that carry the information we're

---

[15] Physical contact is far from necessary, but it is helpful when learning. Later we will learn how to extend an energetic "tendril" to make contact with remote objects, and we can use these same "tendrils" to psychometrize distant objects.

looking for. Emotions, for example, are particularly easy to pick up off of objects when we can feel those emotions arise in our own bodies. Additionally, the etheric field easily imprints onto the astral body. By psychometrizing through etheric contact (by holding the object), we allow ourselves to imprint thoughts and conceptual information onto our own astral body more easily. Thus, in general it's better to hold the object or touch it physically.

Additionally, it should go without saying that we'll be more successful going into the task with a clear mind and without preconceptions about what it is we expect to find. This holds true for all psychic-sensory applications discussed in this book. If we already have beliefs or assumptions about what we will find, then our imagination can get in the way of our ability to sense information. And, without a clear and resting mind, we may not notice the subtle impressions left on our field through contact with an object.

The actual process of psychometry, then, simply involves holding or touching the object and then noticing any changes in our own field. Emotions that arise, concepts that jump suddenly into mind, pictures, images, or symbols are all possible carriers of psychometric information. The skill comes less from sensing these things—everyone can and does, we've all been in a room where a fight has happened and felt uneasy, or held a necklace and recognized the owner—and more from being able to organize this information into a useful format.

The best way to practice, then, is to psychometrize many objects, beginning with those of known qualities. This may seem contrary to the prior advice to avoid things we know about already, but the first steps are to recognize the feelings that arise when we're in contact with specific types of energies. We should know what it "feels like" to hold an object that is imprinted with anger versus one imprinted with calm versus one imprinted with someone's name or some kind of memory or event. Because our energy body determines how these sensations arise in the body and how we perceive them, and because we all have slightly different energy bodies, it's impossible to say how something will appear to everyone. Much psychometric information comes through inner symbolism, as well, and those symbols will also vary from one person to another. So, at first we must hold objects we know about and recognize how those feelings relate to what we know about the object. Then, in the future, when we move onto objects that are unknown, we can recognize those feelings and have a good start.

Once we have developed a large vocabulary of impressions and recognitions, we can move on to objects we don't know about and practice gathering new information from objects. At this point, it remains important to take notes, if only to practice organizing information. The difference between a good psychometric reading and a mediocre one is whether the information is organized in a useful way that people can make sense of.

The opposite of psychometry is *imprinting*, or energetically enchanting an object with qualities, ideas, concepts, or properties. Rather than reading the impressions left objects by others, here we are deliberately making those impressions. This is accomplished by pushing energy onto the object.

Beginning with an object in our hand, simply extend the visualization from before, where we moved energy within the body into our hand. Now, we are pushing the energy out of the hand and into the object, watching the energy form around the object. This process happens naturally in many cases, especially with metals worn on the body or with objects of sentimental value. Simply by contact with our body's natural energy field and through our emotional attention objects can gain the properties of the emotions and ideas we associate to them.

Objects can even carry memories and thoughts with them. Imprinting often happens at times of great trauma or emotional experience, and this is one explanation for many hauntings and so on, where the energy from an emotional experience so strongly imprints onto an object or location that it creates an association others can sense later on. Strong emotions tend to imprint well.

Imprinting also works sympathetically, where certain objects are easier to imprint with certain kinds of emotions, ideas, memories, or so on based on the elemental properties of the material from which it's made. Generally, metals and woods are fairly easy to imprint, taking not much energy or effort but rather readily accepting energetic imprints. Because they tend to have stable and static energetic fields nonorganic, nonmetallic things such as stone or concrete tends to be more difficult to imprint upon, with a notable exception of crystals and so on. Living things, because of their self-determining energetic patterns, also tend to be difficult to imprint as they also create their own pattern which may not be sympathetic to the patterns you are attempting to imprint on them.

With imprinting comes our first exposure also to *patterning*, which is encoding or programming energy with particular ideas, concepts, or emotions which it can then carry into, for example, an object. Returning to our practice, holding a small object in one or both hands, enter your meditative resting state, ground, and center, as usual. Breathing in, draw energy in and begin moving it through the body to your hands. This should be more or less automatic, after having practiced before, and so you can maintain your focus on the object itself. As you exhale, let the energy flow from your hands into the object, and see it merging inseparably into the object and its already existing energy field. This simple process is called *charging* the object, and charging itself only adds your energy to the object. Adding energy yourself will create a sympathetic link with the object, but this does not really constitute imprinting on your own.

To imprint the object, or enchant it, first bring to mind the emotional state or concept you want to imprint. It is best, for emotions, to try to invoke this emotion and actually feel it. For concepts, hold a memory strongly in the mind as concisely as possible and with as little embellishment as possible. As an example, if we wanted to imprint a memory onto an object, we would first recall the memory as vividly as possible. As you do this, visualize that the energy itself takes on the properties of the memory. You can visualize this as the memory melting into the energy and becoming that energy. Then as before, visualize the energy flowing into the object and mixing inseparably with it, carrying with it the concept or idea you're patterning. While we've used the example of a memory here, it can of course be done with any conceptual event: a memory, thought, emotion, feeling, or any other kind of mental object or idea.

Imprinting has a great deal of practical uses, and while it's good for operations to be clean and concise they do not need to be simple as such. We can imprint chairs with good feelings, for example, comfort or invitation, or just general good feelings so as to have a place to go when we want to bring about such emotions. Imprinting such feelings or ideas onto a chair in an office where one conducts business can incline others to be more agreeable. Conversely we might imprint things we don't want people to see with boredom or mundanity, or the general concept of disinterest itself, such that looking at or interacting with the thing inclines a person towards boredom, and encouraging them to move on or not notice the thing at all. A door might be imprinted with the idea of fear or revulsion, keeping would-be visitors away. More advanced applications that border on more traditional magical spellcraft would include imprinting a wallet with the idea of being full or abundant, with the aim of attracting money or financial gain.

The most important aspect in the imprinting of objects is the clarity of the idea we're intending to imprint. Muddled and distracted thinking while forming the intention we wish to imprint will result in a muddled and distracted imprint. A clear impression will mark an object noticeably, but a distracted or unclear imprint will not likely press through a person's other conventional senses. A visually interesting or attractive object may be made unattractive with a clear imprint, but an unclear, distracted enchantment on the same object may not make itself known and will not overcome the obviously sensually attractive qualities.

As I mentioned before, imprinting energy can and does occur naturally even for individuals with no inclination towards subtle energy working. These individuals may suffer from hauntings or curses that are essentially of their own creation. Objects and locations that are so haunted can be disenchanted in a similar way, provided that the effect is indeed being caused by energetic imprinting and not by, for example, some kind of actual spirit inhabitant. In the case of "cursed" objects, those imprinted with a negative or undesirable trait, they can be depatterned in much the same way as they would be imprinted.

With the object in your hand or a safe distance away, concentrate on bringing to mind the kind of unpatterned energy we dealt with earlier, or a kind of chaotic, depatternizing energy that disrupts and dismantles patterned energy. It is suggested in the case of the latter to apply this conditioning *outside* your own body, after you've already pushed your own energy into the object, rather than inside the body, to avoid depatternizing the natural flow of the body's own systems. While the body's physical form will eventually correct the energetic patterning and restore normal function, the disruption to the body's energetic pattern can cause complications. Unlike earlier, where we simply moved energy about, here we are specifically programming energy to behave (or not behave, when depatterning), in a specific way. Doing so within our own bodies can have unwanted consequences. As you direct this depatternizing energy, visualize whatever energetic pattern is already on the object dissolving and disintegrating and the object's energetic pattern returning to a blank state. You may also ground the object directly, pushing its patterned energy out of the object and into the earth where it is dissolved and replaced with unpatterned subtle energy. This is performed the same way as grounding oneself, but rather than directing the energy through our own body, using ourselves as a conduit, we simply push the objects energy into the ground directly.

At this point we have directly worked with energy outside our own body, albeit using the body as a conduit. However, these kinds of effects can also be applied at very long distances. When working a short distance, such as in a room or line of sight, it is a matter of creating a link or channel to the object. Now, we will discuss a method for working over much longer distances.

As usual, in our working state, visualize a tendril or tentacle like conduit of energy reaching off of your own energetic field or aura and touching to the object. Alternatively, this conduit may extend from your hand or fingertips. However you choose to visualize it, see the tendril becoming very concrete but allowing energy to flow through it. Now, just as you pushed the energy from your hand and into the object, push the energy along the tendril and into the object. Tendrils like this are often called *links* or *conduits*, and once they are established they may last for a short or long time, depending on the amount of attention that goes into their creation and your intention when creating it. With some effort, they can even be made somewhat permanent. They are sometimes called *channels*, but this term is more often used to refer to the natural pathways for energy inside the body and so this term can be ambiguous. Links constitute the first real construct we've introduced, and we'll discuss them more throughout this book.

GROUNDING AND CENTERING

Grounding and centering serve as our first application of movement of energy and directing energy flow, and their proximity to our own body makes this an excellent, if perhaps not flashy or exciting, introduction to moving subtle energy. These simple preliminaries may seem unexciting, but will act as force multipliers which dramatically improve the quality of your results moving forward.

Grounding is the first skill where we will employ the idea of visualization, but is aided by appropriate posture. It is best to ground by placing both bare feet on the ground, ideally on the lowest level of a building or outside. It is not *necessary* to be barefooted, but it can help at first by providing a somatic element as well as by providing an unimpeded channel. Though energy can flow through anything, it is often a mental barrier to beginners to see solid objects as too solid for energy to pass through, or to have difficulty mentally instructing this to occur. In any case, the somatic component helps us mentally bridge a "flow path" for directing the energy within our own body. Moving the energy in the "aura" or field surrounding the body around clothing and so on poses little difficulty, but this external energy field merely reflects the energy from inside the body, something like water around a rock.

The counterpart to grounding is *centering*, where we stabilize and calm the energy field internally rather than externally. In this practice we bring all of the energy from the external field into the body, as well as draw energy from the extremities and torso to the central energy point of the body, approximately four inches below the navel. This inward flow is then allowed to flow back out through the central channel, similar to blood moving from veins into the heart and then out through the arteries. This sort of forceful reset reconditions the energy as it passes through the energy center and restores and repairs blockages or incorrect flow through channels. Reconditioning and repatterning this energy can help to purge energetic-emotional feedback loops. Sometimes, due to a strongly felt emotion, we can pattern our own body's energy strongly in such a way that we emanate this emotion. Then, this strongly emotional energy pattern in turn is felt by us, bringing about the strong emotion. This can continue for a long time, essentially until something breaks the loop. Grounding and centering is one very effective and direct way to do so.

Both grounding and centering can be done together, first by drawing the energy to the center, and then by grounding it. This restores our connection to the earth, grounding us more firmly in the material plane, while "dumping" the emotional baggage of patterned energy into the ground and allowing our body to restore itself afresh.

There can sometimes be some confusion when discussing energetic centers, sometimes called *chakras* in the New Age tradition. Coming from the Sanskrit term meaning "wheel," the concept was popularized in the West through the Theosophical society,[16] which borrowed both the term and some understanding of the idea from Indian Yoga Tantra. As is often the case, the concept lost some nuance in the transfer. The Theosophical chakra model generally points to seven or eight chakras and describes them as more or less fixed points in the body with defined, objective purposes within one's spiritual functioning. This is, however, not something that comes from tantra. While chakras do exist in tantra, there is not a single particular number of them, nor is there a fixed mapping of functions. Instead, yogatantra practitioners learn to visualize different numbers of chakras in different positions with different functions for whatever purpose of personal transformation they are aiming to achieve. Sometimes there are two chakras, sometimes four, sometimes seven or eight,

---

[16] C.W. Leadbeater, *The Chakras*, 1927

sometimes hundreds. It all depends on the particular goal being worked towards. The Theosophical model of the chakras certainly *can* work, just as the other models can work, as they are instantiations of abstract concepts and spiritual functions that work through visualization and so on. However, I do not think it's prudent to get in the habit of thinking about chakras like this in some kind of rigid way, as something that is tangibly existent. It is much better to consider such things in a fluid, operative way, related to what one is trying to accomplish at any given time. The common New Age understanding of chakras and their functions is included in an appendix in this book.

Occasionally I may refer to the "energetic center." Here, this means a center of energy a few inches below the navel, where energy can be drawn from. It corresponds to the Sacral Chakra in the theosophical model (see Appendix A), but the location is more or less the end of this relationship. It should be ascribed no special spiritual meaning *in this case*. If in the practice of yoga or tantra you work with the same center, that is fine, and you should use it in those cases according to that tradition. It will not interfere either way, but, in both cases, it is simply representative and purely functional, not an objectively real thing.

Expanding on this, some questions may arise about the nature of the center. If it's not the chakra as described by the theosophists, then what is it, and why address it at all? There are a number of possible answers to this question depending on what is being asked. Primarily, the center exists as a location where there is a significant overlap or connection between the energetic and physical body. The etheric body corresponding to the ganglia and organs that make up the anatomy means there is thick etheric energy readily available here. When working with energy in physical space, this node functions conceptually as a useful reference point. If we are to imagine energy as being related to consciousness, the visceral connection to the physical body in our mind leads energy to assemble here. In any case, it works both conceptually and actually as a tool, regardless of whether this center is thought of as an enduring anatomical structure of the energetic body or simply a reference point of connection of the spiritual body to the physical body. So long as we are focused on working with energy in the physical world around us, such an anchor point is useful.

Assuming the grounded position, standing or sitting with feet shoulder width apart, barefooted, on the ground, visualize the field of energy around yourself like an aura. This aura can be pictured as extending beyond the skin of the body several inches, maintaining the general outline of the human shape, and represents the energy of the body and its function as it emanates out. The aura is essentially the body's subtle energetic field. Like with chakras, there are many traditions that describe auras, and things of various colors and meanings of these colors and so on. Such is especially proper in New Age circles. It is not important to concern yourself at all with the color of the aura or any kind of fixation or focus on it other than to recognize it is there. Aura colors, sizes, and things like this are specific to New Age spirituality and not at all related to the actual working with subtle energy covered in this book. It can be dismissed or adopted at your pleasure.

Your hands can be at your side, or if you prefer to use a kinesthetic component, held loosely in front of the body as if one were carrying a ball roughly the size of a cantaloupe just in front of the navel. Resting the mind in the meditative state, visualize the energy around the body moving about as it naturally does, however you perceive this to be. While breathing in, visualize this energy being drawn into the body and flowing through the body's energetic channels into the center, while raising the hands tightly in front of you towards the chest, keeping the palms open and upwards. As you complete the breath, breathe out and at the same time visualize any 'negative' energy, patterned as it is with undesirable emotions or programming, sickness, or so on down through the feet and into the ground, where it dissipates or is absorbed. At the same time, push downward with both hands. As you breathe in again, turn the hands as if lifting something up again and repeat this process.

There are a few important things to note here. First, I've told you to visualize energy "however you perceive it," which has likely given some pause as most people do not naturally perceive energy in any sense we are used to. We can all, for the most part, naturally sense and perceive energy inasmuch as we are affected by it and can detect that influence. However, some ambiguity in language gives people an expectation of being able to perceive energy as in some conventional sense such as through a biological sense organ. Additionally, the word "visualization" implies a visual process; we're picturing something happening in our minds and at the same time willing that it should happen. Because it is difficult to will something to happen without a kind of perceptual interface, especially at first, we use this visualization to direct our action. This is our first case for developing a "sensory overlay" for energy.

A sensory overlay is a mapping of one sense to another. In this case, we are mapping the sense and perception of subtle energy to a visual idea. However, because there is no way that energy "looks," we choose here our own sensory mapping. Sometimes, for the sake of practice or experimentation, we might program energy to have a "color," but that "color" is information, not an actual wavelength of light, and so while energy might be mapped "blue" or "purple" or whatever we choose, it does not really possess that *quality* so much as it possesses that *information*. Similarly, we will naturally have some kind of visual that comes to mind when someone says "picture a subtle energy field" or "mentally visualize the energy moving from point A to point B." Here we get to assign that association for the first time. However we see that, whatever mental image comes to mind, we can use to create this sensory overlay. It is important to note that the movement of the energy may or may not be exactly that same way, but language being what it is it is usually fairly consistent. When we say energy "flows" from one place to another, this describes an activity, if not in specific detail, but the idea of "flowing" as opposed to, say, "zapping" or "rushing" or even "streaming" is distinctive enough that we can all get mostly the same idea. Our visualizations do not need to be similar to other people's visualizations so long as the common language term we would use to describe the action is similar enough. Some people prefer to visualize energy as electrical, and its flow is like that of electricity through pipes or like electromagnetic waves. Others prefer to visualize it as like water, or like the movement of wind or air. Still others associate it with fire. When working with elemental energy, our visualizations change to adapt to this. But all of these are fine, and whatever method we prefer is fine.

As for the perception of energy, this comes from practice in visualization and working with energy. As we work with energy, our sense for it becomes more acute the way we might develop a more acute taste for wine on our way from becoming a casual drinker of wine to a sommelier. As our sense for energy improves through practice and familiarity with it, our sensory overlay or visual mapping will also adapt to be more discriminating, and our visualizations will change slightly over time, coming in finer detail to reflect subtlety, and corresponding more and more closely to how the energy actually moves naturally. Most people have some sense for energy automatically: that sensation we get when we walk through a graveyard long since overgrown, or the feeling of piety in a building that, unbeknownst to us, used to be a church, or the feeling "off" when we handle the charm once belonging to a person that feels ever so slightly, but tangibly different from the same charm when we see it in the store. The key here is not to struggle to learn to perceive energy as if this is some radical shift, but to instead simply allow ourselves to trust and rely on senses we already have, and thereby improve them.

Another important point is that the visualization in this case is not merely how we want things to be, but begins with visualizing how things *are*. We begin the practice by entering the undistracted meditative state we've been working on, so that we do not bring our own baggage or expectations to the initial visualization. This allows us to start that visualization based on a correspondence of the physical state we are mindfully aware of with the energetic state as it rests prior to our working. It is entirely possible to simply begin visualizing the energy in the state we'd like, and then let it figure itself out as it gets there, but in these early stages of learning it is more important to develop a sense for the energy and how it moves, and for the purposes of grounding and centering it is counterproductive to start off the exercise by visualizing things a mess and then fixing it when we may not be that big a mess to begin with. For this reason, we want to begin by feeling for how things are, and visualizing the energy first in a state that we can reasonable believe is how it actually is, despite our lack of direct sensation.

What begins as a symbolic association to our mental visualization of movement of energy ends up as a symbolic association that directly reflects the state of energy that while not imperceptible is usually perceived more through a vaguely emotional or conceptual sense than in strictly concrete or material sensation. By creating this symbolic association as a sensory overlay we can instantiate energy rather than working with it in very abstract terms, and this can help us organize what we intend to do.

Related to this organization is the incorporation of physical motions into the working of energy. Practitioners of internal martial arts such as Tai Chi or Baguazhang will recognize some movements as related to their own martial practice. Even where they do not, they already know that energy can be moved about the body through physical action alone. Incorporating the physical action into the work not only serves as a natural method of manipulating energy within the body, but as another sensory modality which we can recruit to make the work more concrete. When we do this, abstract ideas become more focused, and this assists us in planning and directing energy with precision. If we want to move energy to a (relatively) fixed point in space, that is easy enough, but it can be made much easier if we, for example, use our hand to position it where we'd like, or anchor it to a physical object. By placing our hands on a person, we can directly bridge energy from one system to another, and create a conduit that is very easy to direct energy along. By using our hands to simulate rising and falling, we not only facilitate the movement of energy through the body but we remind ourselves what the action should feel like.

This incorporation of physical motions is not entirely necessary, but serves to assist in the early stages of practice. It does not need to be abandoned to advance further, but it does help in the beginning as well as when working with others. For example, if two people are moving energy to the same relatively fixed point, having a physical indicator and using a physical motion can help ensure that both people are focusing on the same actual point.

It also serves to recruit another sense into the work, which can improve our focus and prevent distraction. As we move about physically we are less prone to let our mind wander, as our focus on the physical aspect of the work serves to keep our focus on the movement of energy and prevents us from moving on to thinking about lunch.

Lastly, this use of physical actions, when repeated the same way over and over, can serve to create *cantrips*, a kind of magical shorthand. Historically, the word "cantrip" comes from

Gaelic where it can refer to any kind of illusion or spell. In modern usage, a cantrip is a spell that can be easily cast due to extensive practice and familiarity, which is "cast" by performing a well-practiced and rehearsed shorthand action. A cantrip is therefore effectively a trained signal to oneself which, when used, triggers caster to perform the desired psychic or magical effect automatically. In addition to the utility of training ourselves to quickly perform specific actions without having to first collect ourselves and focus our full attention, cantrips can be used to abbreviate spells and workings that involve multiple steps or complicated processes into a more manageable work that takes less concentration. While this is not really necessary for, for example, grounding and centering, and while it comes with its own set of drawbacks, it will become more useful as we move on to more advanced workings, and will be discussed in more detail then.

Centering works hand in hand with grounding. When we discharge the contaminated, poorly imprinted energy into the ground and draw clean, pure energy back in, we can use this to re-imprint it to how it should be. This is something like hitting the factory reset. Here is where the chakra model becomes somewhat more useful. Different chakras can be used in centering to resolve different problems with different aspects of the energy body.

Chakras are conceptual tools representing the intersection of functions of different parts of the body. Important ones with which most people are familiar are the root chakra, sacral chakra, solar plexus chakra, and third eye chakra. The root chakra is the intersection between the etheric body and the physical body. The sacral is the interface between the near-astral and etheric body. The remaining chakras serve intersecting function in the mental astral body. The solar plexus chakra, for example, governs our sense of ego and identity. Centering to the solar plexus, therefore, helps us find "us," while centering to the root chakra helps us resynchronize the etheric body to the physical. These specific functions are addressed in Appendix A.

Grounding and centering are important skills that will continue to be used throughout this book, and should ideally be done before any kind of working, in conjunction with entering into the meditative resting state of concentration.

CONSTRUCTS

Now that we have practiced moving energy outside the body or in any physical objects, we can begin working with energy simply in space. Energy does not need to inhabit a physical form, but can exists in parallel to physical things, occupying the same space. It can also occupy empty space, air, water, and so on, irrespective of the medium. In some applications, it is useful to build an *energetic construct*, a shape or form of energy that does not occupy an object but rather simply exists in a location. Energetic constructs can be any shape or size one desires, with varying density or solidity. In fact, we've already made our first energetic construct by way of the link we established earlier for charging and imprinting objects.

Beginning as usual, choose a point in space. For many, it is easiest to choose a point between our two hands, held in space as if holding a baseball. Focusing on this point, breathing in, draw energy up and out of the energetic center, and then, while exhaling, visualize this energy flowing out of the palms of the hands into the space between. As the energy flows to the point, visualize it accumulating there at that point, growing larger and larger. If it grows so large as to push against the hands, you may feel sensations similar to moving energy within the body. You can move the hands further apart, then bring them together, smashing the ball denser and denser as desired. This exercise, often called a *psiball* in various online communities, is many people's first introduction to energy work.

On the introductory level, these kinds of shaped constructions are mainly for practice, but because we have already worked with imprinting and programming objects we already know there are other applications through patterning. We can program the energy in this space to make one feel warm or cool, to soothe or cause pain, to relax or excite, and so on.

Let's go back to the psiball. As you add energy to the area, consider altering its shape. Consider visualizing a cube, or pyramid, or any other three-dimensional object into which to move this energy, charging the area. The clarity of your visualization will determine how accurately the energy can move into this pattern and how stably it will maintain the form. This, again, emphasizes the importance of meditative concentration and the ability to maintain focus. However, at this point it may become useful to begin exercising your clarity of visualization. This can generally be done by imagining scenes of varying complexity and greater and greater detail. Imagining yourself at a festival, think about what you see. For each character or thing that you imagine, picture greater and greater detail. Visualization, like any other skill, needs practiced, and imagining scenes of increasingly great complexity challenges our ability to maintain clarity in complex imagery. This exercise can be paired with meditative concentration and then brought directly to our energy work as one creates constructs of increasingly sophisticated detail.

That said, there is little point to such sophistication in the material plane. It becomes much more useful as we progress forward to work in the astral. It also helps us in learning to shape energy, which can be useful as greater focus and emphasis on even simple constructions can increase their longevity and stability.

Naturally, small handsized objects are not the only objects we can create. Two-dimensional energetic planes can be used to demark thresholds or areas one does not wish to be crossed, placed in doors, and so on and programmed however one chooses: to deter people from entry, or encourage it, or to induce certain emotions as one crosses through, or so on. Larger fields, much like our own energetic field which surrounds us, can be placed in rooms or areas to the same effect. Someone seeking privacy may make an entire room disinteresting to be in by filling the room with an energy that is programmed to discourage anyone therein.

Moving into more directly magical applications, we can also program energy with desired outcomes. We might surround a basketball hoop with a greater likelihood for baskets, or a reduced likelihood, depending on our whims. This kind of energetic imprinting meant to encourage or discourage possible outcomes is often known as *probability alteration*. One might also deploy a strongly imprinted area attractive to, for example, spirits, or policemen, or whatever one wants. These overtly magical processes can also be accomplished through other types of magic, but can in this way be accomplished through subtle energy manipulation. This kind of work is also improved if the desired outcome can be visualized strongly and particularly, or if the desired outcome is already one which frequently occurs in the area, or so on.

Constructs can also be used to train in sensing with popular exercises where two people can take turns making constructs then assessing their shape, "color," imprinted emotions, and so on. Consider using different sensory modalities for your sensory overlays, rather than just visual information. Particularly worth consideration would be the sense of touch, feeling out the shapes and information, and proprioception, our innate sense of locational-positional information.

As always, after having built constructs and worked with imprinting and programming, ground and center to restore your field's natural balance.

The size and sophistication of any given construct is not limited by the subtle energy itself, but by a number of other factors. As we've discussed, sources of energy are effectively infinite, and "exhausting" energy from a source is uncommon, so the limitations do not come from resources. Instead, they come from the functional bandwidth of our own mind and our ability to concentrate, as well as the nature of energy itself and how it corresponds to the physical environment and tends to dissipate over time. By developing our mental faculties through meditation, we can reduce the limitations of bandwidth by increasing our ability to sustain attention on multiple tasks. Here we are not trying to focus intently, necessarily, but rather directing the energy and maintaining our awareness of it as we "allow" it to take shape. This comes with practice.

The other limiting factor, that of a kind of energetic entropy where constructs will dissipate as they are exposed to other imprinting or to correspondent factors from either the material or astral planes that diminish their imprinting or create new imprints, are mitigated by sustained attention and by building the construct well and strongly, devoting the same kind of strong imprinting we discussed in that chapter to the construct. The more powerful the intention and the stronger the projection of it, the longer the construct will last. By bringing our attention back to it and reinforcing the imprint occasionally, we can make it more resilient to counter-programming. Neither of these tasks are trivial to do, and it should not be surprising if it takes some time to do so. Fortunately, the more often we build a construct, the easier it becomes to bring our attention to the task and the less effort it takes to focus on it.

Many people will focus on trying to develop increasingly elaborate constructs. This is a noble goal if we have something to accomplish, but can quickly get out of hand and actually lead to us getting much worse at working with subtle energy. The goal is to move energy about through visualization, and this does not require sophisticated visualizations to accomplish. Instead, the humble psi ball is an excellent tool of practice. What we must work on is strengthening the association between our visualization and the movement of energy. The movement of energy on its own as a result of our visualization is minimal, simply a result of the gentle push of the astral body as the mind focuses towards something.

The skill we must develop is having energy respond quickly and powerfully to those directions of will. We do not accomplish this by strengthening our ability to visualize. That is also an important task, but it won't help our energy work *per se*. Instead, we must strengthen the association between visualization and action. For this, making strong, stable, dense constructs quickly through act of will is a far better exercise. By observing the process as we do it, being honest with ourselves, taking notes, and making constructs close enough to us within our etheric field that we can physically feel the results, we can actually develop our skill. Otherwise, we can quickly find ourselves in self-delusion, visualizing grand and elaborate constructs that we do not fully form, and without the sensitivity to recognize that we are not succeeding.

The humble psiball" then, is one of the best ways of practicing. Here we want to focus on density, shape, and rapidity of response. We want to differentiate the feelings in our body that come from the motions we associate with making a psiball and focus on making the construct. Our perceptions of this are our best tool for recognizing a success. More rapid production of the psiball, in a denser, more compact form, with all of the associated feelings of success, are the goal. We can do this with others to verify the task is done, though this is best done with a partner in person. We should not restrict our practice only to when others are available to help, however. Creating constructs is something we can and should do on our own, using partners or teachers to verify our progress, but not to verify our success at any given time after we've demonstrated that we're able to do it.

We never need to "move on" past a psiball, just as a basketball player never "moves on" from practicing free throws and a guitarist never "moves on" from practicing scales. What begins as something we must learn to do becomes something we do to warm up. Creating a ball of energy is different from creating a ball of energy *perfectly*, in perfect accordance with our will. So, we should practice the psi ball frequently, every day, several times a day. We should make sure to take frequent breaks, especially after successes, to allow our unconscious mind the time to organize the processes that resulted in a success.

ENERGETIC HYGIENE AND DISSOLUTION

Once we have begun working with projecting energy consciously around the body and making constructs, it is inevitable that we're going to start leaving things around. Programmed energy disrupts the natural flow of energy in rooms and locations. These disruptions, essentially energetic clutter, can lead to the development of the same kind of clutter physically, as well as to dampened emotions and mental fatigue. They can also be disruptive to the practice of subtle energy work as previous programming mixes into and interferes with our own. Additionally, as we are working with moving energy around the body, occasionally we can develop difficult areas of disrupted energetic flow and damaged energetic fields.

We have already discussed grounding and centering, which help to mitigate these problems within the body. However, sometimes these clumps of energy do not break up and move away on their own or through grounding or centering. For this, we have *scraping* and *rattling*. The latter, rattling, is named for one of the more effective tools for the job: a baby's rattle or otherwise musical rattle. Shaking these rattles, the sound can depattern strongly clumped up energy. While not a guarantee to dissolve all constructs, it will break up energy that is not "flowing" due to eddies in a room, impediments to flow, or having been depatterned of its dynamism. When done around the body, it can depatternize clumped up or stagnant energy which dulls the field and our sensitivity.

Rattling is often accompanied with scraping, again named for exactly what it is. Usually this is done by charging the hands and then simply scraping up, picking up the energy that is causing the problem and disposing of it either through grounding or by placing the energy into a bowl of salt. When scraping, one does not need to physically touch the person. Instead scraping the field with the hands about an inch from their skin suffices. Personally, I like to combine rattling and scraping by doing this in the shower, where the cascading water can effectively simulate the role of the rattle and the drain serves as a reasonable disposable for the clumped up, stagnant energy.

When scraping others, using both hands, start from the top of the head on either side of it, working down from shoulder to hands and over the tips of the fingers, then down the torso and each leg separately, always working from the head down, and from the torso out along limbs, from the shoulders to the fingers and from the hips to the toes. This reduces the possibility of recontaminating already cleaned areas and pushes negative energy away from the sensitive head and central nervous system in the correct and natural directions, flowing away from the central channels. After the head and each limb, as well as the torso, dispose of anything that has been scraped away into salt or wherever you're disposing of the energy.

When scraping oneself, the process is the same, using the right hand to scrape above and below the left arm and vice versa, then using both hands for each leg like pulling off a pair of pants. With some practice this can be done quickly and easily. Scraping often leaves people feeling "lighter" the first time they have it done, as many people are coated in loads of psychic residue accumulated over many years. After the first time, the change will feel less dramatic usually, and unless a person becomes contaminated again through exposure to psychically filthy areas, it may take some time before the same amount of stagnant energy can accrue. If scraping and rattling are performed regularly the field will stay light and clean which will improve sensitivity and functionality.

A rattle need not necessarily be exactly a rattle. It is the dynamism and the static, unpatterned nature of the instrument that lends itself to the purpose and so other things including actual static or white noise can be effective. Additionally, instruments like bells can cut through stagnated energetic patterning, and purifying incenses or things like smudges (a preparation of smoke used by various magical sorts for purifying or cleaning areas) can also help. A rattle, however, can easily be made at home with almost anything, and so becomes very convenient for the purpose.

We do not need to spend a lot of time trying to make an area completely devoid of subtle energy. A room will naturally have a flow of energy and it is perfectly fine – good, even – to leave that flow in place. Instead, what we want to avoid are stagnant areas where energy pools. As energy flows through a room, it naturally clears away its own patterning and imprinting, defaulting through correspondence to essentially whatever is going on there in the material or astral. A living room will have the energy of a living room without our interference, and when we clean away whatever is there it will quickly be restored as a living room.

In rooms with poor energetic flow, however, whatever incidental imprinting occurs can linger for some time and ultimately begin changing the astral and material conditions of the room. A stagnant room where energy has pooled after, for example, a fight, will continue to harbor that angry and aggressive energy. This is the case where attention should be paid to cleaning the room in particular.

It is also worthwhile to consider employing basic concepts of interior design which can facilitate energy flow. Some concepts of *feng shui* can be borrowed here for good energetic movement. For example, we should avoid empty nooks and strong right angles in rooms whenever possible, instead positioning furniture to allow a flow path for energy. Reflective baubles or colorful, moving things can break stagnation in corners of rooms, as can clever employment of light. Mirrors reflect energy as they do light, so they should not be placed across from doors or windows so as to avoid them reflecting back whatever energy comes in and leaving the rest of the room stagnant. Moving water, such as from a small table fountain, can also help facilitate movement of energy. At a glance, areas where dust or dander accumulate are also areas where energetic detritus will likely accumulate, and these areas are where we should focus our attention when cleaning a room.

As your ability to sense energy improves, you will be able to assess for yourself the movement of energy in a room. Stagnant rooms feel heavier and are weighted with emotions and thoughts that do not always seem appropriate to the area. They may also feel stifled or "blocked up" and static. Once you can clearly sense this energetic stagnation, it will no longer be necessary to rely entirely on these rules of thumb, as you will be able to come up with them for yourself, identifying the problem areas and fixing them as necessary.

With constructs, it is also possible to create things like energetic cleaning robots which can take care of the space without your direct involvement, even sustaining themselves off of the static energy they consume. Because these constructs do not need complicated forms, even a simple psiball can serve, along with the imprinting to clean or dissolve stagnated energy, or the concept of scraping itself. It is important, here, to make sure that we imprint and encode the construct with the intention of performing the action, and not the action itself, lest we dissolve it in creation.

ENERGETIC HEALING AND AURA READING

One of the more common and in fact mainstream uses for energy work is as a form of alternative medicine. I don't think that there is ever a case in which energetic healing, from the very basic level taught here, to the most advanced forms of traditional energy healing methods, are a substitute for the proper and judicious application of allopathic medicine. Still, the use of energy to soothe a headache, ache, or pain, or to assist in the palliation of injuries or illnesses, can be very useful. Here we can employ both imprinting and constructs together to help others directly.

The most basic technique for helping others with pain or illness through subtle energy manipulation is essentially to help them to ground, center, and scrape themselves, or to do so for them. This can remove the conglomerated energy that they have naturally imprinted with the sensations of pain or illness, which creates energetic space for healing to occur. It sometimes may alleviate pain and discomfort in and of itself, especially in individuals known to be more sensitive to subtle energy. In any case, it is good practice to rattle, scrape, ground, and center anyone when working on them with subtle energy, as it reduces the possibility of interference from psychic detritus. When scraping someone with pain or illness, we should focus especially on the affected area but we should not neglect to scrape the entire body. Some discretion should be used in rattling. A person complaining of a migraine headache, for example, may not appreciate the noise, and this step might be omitted for that reason.

Once we have performed the preparatory work of cleaning the person's energetic field, we can move to focusing on caring for their actual complaint. For the sake of an example, we will discuss healing here primarily focusing on things like headaches, minor wounds, pain associated with illness, and so on. As in all palliative care, the focus here is on reducing pain and increasing comfort, not on actually healing the disease. The reason for this is that the disease process can be very complex, and without a proper understanding of what we are doing, it is certainly possible to hurt someone or make things worse. Essentially, when treating someone with subtle energy, we are still treating someone, and there is no reason to imagine that because our intentions are good, we can do no harm!

Counterintuitively, at this level, it is actually better to have a very non-specific and deliberately vague intention for healing or reducing pain. It is best not to focus specifically on anatomical details, how pain is transferred along synapses, and so on. Instead, it is better to create wards or constructs which are imprinted with an energy intended to reduce pain. By asking for the person to qualify their pain, we can tailor this specifically to address that sensation. A burning pain we would want to treat by filling the area with cooling energy, where a stinging pain we may want to counter with a soothing. Imprinting merely the absence of pain may help, but imprinting a sensation that counteracts the one the person is experiencing is most likely to be successful. We do not want to get into anatomical detail because it is again possible to hurt someone by inducing their body to function in a way it should not. This can inhibit healing, or, at worst, make things much worse.

The actual process of moving this energy is similar to how we've discussed before. After going through the steps to clean the person's field, calming our minds, focus on the intent of the construct we want to create. As an example, let's say our friend has a bad headache. Here, we can focus on a cooling sensation. If they report the headache as "stabbing," we can mentally conceive of the sensation of the stabbing implement being "pulled out." Importantly, in this case, we don't want to do something like "visualize a knife in their head coming out," but instead we simply want to create the sensation, imagining what that would feel like and then "visualizing" *that*. With this palliative sensation firmly in our mind, we can set about moving the energy from whatever our source is, or from our own energetic center, through the hands, and out to the person's head.

Now, we have options. Having scraped their energetic field, we know that it is unlikely, for now, to have a lot of detritus or to have been re-imprinted by their own thoughts and feelings and so on. We can now either imprint their energetic field with the desired sensation, directly focusing it in the area around their head. Or, alternatively, we can build a construct, like a cooling helmet, which reduces pain. When going the route of the construct, we already have strong symbolic associations that we can employ to strengthen it. For example, we might visualize a bandaid or bandage over an injury, which we imprint with the appropriate pain reducing sensations. For the head, a helmet is a good option.

It is best in this case to keep such constructs out of the physical body, rather applying them to the surface of the body or the energetic field. When we work with constructs inside the body, while the likelihood of injury is low, it is much higher than the potential benefits would warrant. Firstly, pain is often referred when it originates from points inside the body, and isn't actually coming from the source of the injury. Secondly, the body itself is full of sensitive bits, and working with energy inside it can cause things to go wrong. For the same reason we don't try to focus on ameliorating pain by reducing the function of the nervous system, it's best to not work with energy inside someone's body without a very good understanding of energetic anatomy. This kind of practice is certainly possible, but requires a higher level of training than I will provide here. For the energetic healer who wishes to do more and better, Reiki, Therapeutic Touch, or Emotional Freedom Technique are all good places to start.

It's also possible to encourage healing through application of vague constructs. Again, we want these to be non-specific. Healing is something the body does very well on its own and in its own time. We should not try to accelerate processes or so on, but rather we can simply apply a construct with the concept of healing itself in place. Doing anything more specific runs the risk of making things worse despite all good intentions. Like all medical care, it is important to either know very well what we are doing, or not do it and only work within our level of care. While we can offer some healing as a supplement to an injury, or reduce pain, or so on, it would be foolhardy to try to stitch flesh directly just as it would be reckless to attempt to apply stitches on one's own without training. The healing-facilitative energetic construct or ward, however, is unlikely to cause harm so long as it is specifically just healing facilitative and not attempting to get too specific.

Aura reading is a related practice to healing, as it is often used by energy workers to diagnose maladies or areas of focus. It is also a useful skill for those in the business of helping others with their energetic hygiene. In addition to physical and energetic health, the aura can also *generally* give us a little information about a person's personality and temperament.

At its most basic, aura reading is psychometry as applied to a person's energy body rather than to an object's energy field. Most people, when they discuss an aura, are referring to the local field around a person, comprised of the etheric body, the etheric field, and the astral-emotional body. The aura, then, extends about 2-3 feet from a person's body, with greater density around the body itself and less density as the field fades out into the astral.

Like psychometry, much of the practice involves inner symbolism. Though popular in New Age circles, we cannot really use charts of aura "color" to determine emotional state or spiritual development. It is certainly possible that we might perceive an aura as possessing a "color," but the colors are not properties of the energy body itself. Rather, they are a symbolic perception that occurs in our mind. Where I might see a blue aura, another person may see indigo, or white, or so on. The color comes from the information on the field. Similarly, we cannot use the associated colors with the standard theosophical chakra system to determine someone's level of spiritual development. These structures are far from universal, and it is much better to determine our own symbolic systems through practice and experience.

However, there are some general rules that can be applied when reading an aura. These are not universal either, of course. An experienced subtle energy worker can change the presentation of his or her aura, for example. What would be a very expansive aura might appear quite constrained due to the presence of a shield. Still, as a general rule these properties can be applied in looking at the aura.

First is expansiveness versus constriction. As a general rule, positive emotional states lead the emotional-astral body to expand, as it is more receptive. Extraversion, conscientiousness, and agreeableness[17] also generally lead to an expanded field. The opposite is also true: introverts, people who don't care about others, or people who don't get along with others will have constricted fields. Happy, more energetic people will tend to have brighter fields, while depressed or tired people will have less vibrant fields.

---

[17] One of the main psychological tools for looking at personality is the "Big Five" or "OCEAN" list of personality characteristics. The "Big Five" are openness to new experiences, conscientiousness, extraversion, agreeableness, and neuroticism. This system of personality characteristics is unique in that it is highly validated by statistical models; whereas other systems, like the Myers-Briggs Typology Indicator (MBTI), are less well supported.

Neurotic individuals will often have more "active," chaotic fields. The movement will be substantial as thoughts give rise to emotions. This can also lead to a "brightness," but of a different quality. Here we highlight the distinction between how people see things, as I can't really explain the distinction. Experience will have to be your guide in the difference between a vibrant field from happiness and a vibrant field from neurosis.

On the other hand, experienced meditators, calm people, and those without worries or concerns will often have still fields. These people will tend to feel better to be around generally, aura reading aside. Their auras are like an oasis of calm in an otherwise chaotic world. This is regardless of any kind of symbolic association like color. Rather, the field is calm because the mind is calm and at rest. When the mind is at rest, the energies slow themselves down, leading to stability. In turn, the stable energies resist agitation, leading to a stable state of emotional rest.

Color associations will vary from reader to reader, though those who are heavily invested in a particular system will organize their inner symbolism around that system. Thus many aura readers will associate color with "active chakra." This is in itself a symbolic association, as we've already discussed how chakras are conceptual associations that are perceived though not necessarily present.

Rudolf Steiner suggested looking for active chakras to determine spiritual advancement, but of course this only works if the aura reader sees chakras; and the aura reader may only see chakras because he or she is organizing general information about the energy field symbolically into chakras, which our mind can make better sense of than just raw information. So too, color association is largely culturally bound on the part of the percipient. Two people may read the same aura as different colors not because the aura possesses "color," but because their cultural symbolism identifies the person's personal qualities with different colors. Red may represent anger to one person, lust to another, and good fortune to a third.

WARDS AND DEFENSIVE CONSTRUCTS

The actual need for warding and psychic self-defense is often debated, with opinions varying from the view that it is almost never necessary, merely an artifact of paranoia, to the view that it is an essential first skill for an aspiring energy worker to learn. In my opinion, the need for shielding varies too widely on a case to case basis to be universally mandated one way or another. On the one hand, first time energy workers and especially first time astral projectors often find themselves in contact with local spirits and so on. This is often the result of being noticed as making contact by local spirits. It is often the case, especially today, that many people ignore or otherwise do not regard the needs or wants of spirits in the physical world, and so when spirits find someone who is capable of hearing their concerns they make an effort to make themselves known. In the past this was often the role of the shaman, a particular spiritual practitioner for a village, tribe, or so on that took personal responsibility to serve as the conduit between the spiritual and material realms.

Because of this potential for contact, first time energy workers may find themselves with a whole slew of new experiences for which they may be ill equipped, and in this case shielding and warding may provide some respite from strange experiences. It should be noted that while such encounters with spirits are not *usually* harmful, the possibility does exist, and so some caution should always be demonstrated when communicating with spirits, much as one should demonstrate caution when meeting a stranger in a strange land. These skills are also particularly useful for children who demonstrate psychic aptitude, as spirits do not often recognize the difference between children and adults in these situations and still consider them a potential contact. Shielding and warding can also protect telepathic and empathic children from the problems associated with those conditions, helping to draw a delineation between one's own thoughts and feelings and those of others.

While both are defensive constructs, the difference between a *shield* and a *ward* is the form and method by which they go about their tasks. A *ward* is a general field that exerts its influence over an area. For example, one might ward a room against telepathic activity, and thereby dampen telepathic activity in the entire area. A shield, on the other hand, is a more physical kind of construct. For example, a barrier which blocks telepathic contact, or which prevents external energy from coming into contact with the person inside it. Shields and wards both come in a variety of forms and sizes. Shields are typically built as actual barriers which may be either stationary or mobile, while wards are often used on either areas or with focus objects which carry the effect around as a field.

Perhaps the most common type of shield is the bubble, which resembles force fields in science fiction. Forming a bubble shield can be done any number of ways, and perhaps no two people really visualize them the same way. At this point, it is important that we begin developing our own visualizations to more directly engage with our own unconscious mind in order to mobilize the energy in the way we intend. Nevertheless, for the purposes of training I will provide one here. You can use this, or any other visualization which symbolically represents and communicates your intentions.

Entering the meditative state and focusing on a point in front of you, with or without your hands as a physical focus, draw energy from your energetic center and, exhaling, visualize this energy flowing to the point in space you have chosen via tendrils as discussed before. Continue this process until the energy is dense and glowing. As more and more energy is added, visualize the point expanding now into a sphere, and that sphere growing larger and larger. As the sphere of energy grows larger, move it to surround the object you intend to shield. Then, visualize the energy forming a hollow shell around the object, anchored to it by tendrils. Adding more energy, visualize this shield becoming very solid, a barrier which other external energy moves around. Other energy sent at the shield may be absorbed by it, moved around it, or simply pass through from one side to the other without ever coming through the hollow center. How you choose to visualize and build this depends on the task you want for the shield.

To imprint or program it, first have the intention of the shield firmly in your mind before you begin moving the energy. It is possible to build the shield first, and then program it later, but it is certainly cleaner and more effective to have the energy imprinted with the desired outcome as it is being drawn out from your energetic center.

You may choose to imprint a shield to prevent energy from coming in towards you, but not from going out from you. Such a shield would reduce the influence of energetic imprinting but may also significantly dampen your energetic "senses," making it difficult to sense outside the bubble. You may attune this imprinting to block certain kinds of energetic signals, such as telepathic or empathic or sensory information which could be disturbing, or the "white noise" of telepathic static in crowded places which results from so many people patterning the energy around them with passive thought. Some people are more prone to patterning energy and impressing thoughts, called projective telepaths, and this will be discussed later in the chapter on communication. This kind of shield can also be programmed to guard against other forms of telepathic intrusion.

Warding is essentially an identical process to the imprinting of an area or object, but with specific intentions to drive away or be repulsive to certain things or to prevent or diminish the effects of things within its area. For example, one might ward a piece of jewelry to protect against telepathic information, charging it with energy to expand its field of effect to the area around it without creating a solid barrier that might be penetrated. Or, one might charge a room with a field of energy which is repulsive to spirits or even people, either with the purpose of altering the probability that one might enter, or to make it unremarkable or disinteresting to enter, or even strictly to make spirits or so on feel urgently like they must leave. These kinds of wards affect entire areas generally, and so the effect may be more intense than a shield which, once breached, will no longer serve as an effective defense. Of course, both shields and wards may be combined. When combining the two, a shield prevents specific things from entering, and a ward makes it more difficult for those things to enter if the shield fails.

Because wards tend to create energetic fields, they are often better for the purposes of dampening or restricting psychic "noise," whereas shields are more equivalent to the defensive perimeters often established when doing magical work. A shield can be worked within, whereas a ward affects everyone within its area regardless. It is, of course, possible to program a ward to not affect certain people, but this is a difficult and more advanced process requiring very clear intentions and being more complicated it is certainly possible for this to go wrong in ways we might not anticipate. Shields are certainly simpler to program if we intend to be working inside a perimeter and especially if we intend to have others working with us.

For children with innate sensitivities to telepathy or empathy, it is worth consideration to make them a sort of "safe space" free from energetic interference where they can go when overloaded. This should, of course, be done with their input and consent, as otherwise it can be seen as akin to blindfolding them. Such a ward might keep out non-physical entities, dampen telepathic input or output, or many other possible uses. Naturally such things can be used by adults as well. This can be coupled with, for example, "comfort fields" which generate good feelings and serve as a great way for people who work with the public to isolate themselves and clean off the detritus of the day and the overstimulation from telepathic contact.

Returning to the topic of cantrips, shields and wards are one of the first major applications where a cantrip would very useful. It's hard to imagine a need for an arbitrary shape to be something we'd need to produce quickly and without great mental effort, and while grounding and centering are common applications they really aren't complicated enough to warrant forming a cantrip. Firmly forming an intention for a shield, a structure, and the small ritual by which we would trigger it, we can make an easily deployable shield cantrip to serve whatever purpose we might find expedient, be it shielding telepathic information or just making us less (or more) noticeable in public, or whatever it is we need.

We can also combine this cantrip with several others to make a kind of simplistic ritual. Rituals are not uncommon in the general magical and religious sphere and in fact we all generally perform a variety of rituals in the day. Our daily habits and routines are a form of ritual. When we bring multiple cantrips together to create a ritual, we train ourselves to perform an activity that helps us when we may not be focused or have the presence of mind to organize our thoughts. A ritual brings us to the state of mind where we want to be through habit and repetition. We may be upset, or distracted, but when we perform the ritual, associative memory can calm us down and put us in the working state. Additionally, with practice and repetition, the ritual can also bring about the effect we're aiming to achieve in the same way a cantrip can be used as shorthand to accomplish a mental task without going fully through the steps. In essence, with cantrips, we allow our subconscious mind to take care of the steps, and with a ritual, we bring about the mindset we need to accomplish this as well.

Rituals might be used to defend ourselves when we are doing some kind of magical working, when we are in a strange environment that makes concentration difficult, when we are being actively and adversely affected by an unwanted influence, or just to help us organize our working with energy. In fact, working with ritual is one of the most effective ways to ensure we achieve consistent results. A ritual does not need to be some kind of magical incantation or trance, or even to use ceremonial tools, candles, and so on. A ritual can be a simple pattern of motions, a series of mental activities, or any other routine behaviors. I suggest developing a combination of mental and physical activities for rituals as using our physical body in the work helps keep us grounded in the physical plane and gives us something to focus on. Utilizing multiple media or sensory modalities can help focus and hone our attention.

Of course, there are many times that performing an elaborate ritual may not be viable. We may be in public, or we may not have time or materials on hand. We can also condense rituals themselves down to cantrips, but this requires us to be extremely familiar with the ritual. The bottom line with cantrips and rituals both is that we reinforce them by practicing them as well as by practicing the thing we are abbreviating. We cannot simply make a shield, assign a cantrip, and expect this to work every time. We must be able to make such a shield effectively on our own, and only then can we dismiss the handling of it to the subconscious mind. Like an athlete who has practiced a technique thousands of times, and then can perform it flawlessly even under duress while making it seem effortless, we need to extensively practice skills we would choose to perform in abbreviated forms like cantrips or rituals.

Another potential use for shields or wards is to notify us when others come or go through the field. To do this, we can program the shield or ward to give us a telepathic or energetic "ping" when they are passed through. This "ping" can be either an energetic signal, if we are at a stage in our perceptive skills where such would get our attention, or a telepathic message sent via energetic means. Let's now take a look at methods of communication using energy.

So far, we have only discussed this kind of psychic defense in terms of contact with spirits, hostile magicians, or unwanted thoughts, but it is not the only kind of defense for which shields and wards can be employed. In fact, the most common kind of psychic attack today is marketing and advertising, and the pernicious influence of memes, logos, catchphrases, soundbites, and the like. These kinds of informational influences aim to affect our behavior through thought control, though we rarely use such dramatic language for them. They are, nevertheless, essentially magical sigils meant to compel or influence us in certain ways. We can shield ourselves from these influences or ward them off just as we might any other kind of psychic attack. Building a shield for example that protects someone from the psychic influence associated with brands or corporate logos can help one to ignore these kinds of subtle thought-magic which have become so strongly a part of our culture.

COMMUNICATION: TELEPATHY AND EMPATHY

Telepathy and empathy are two of the skills most people immediately associate with psychics generally, and empathy is perhaps one of the more commonly accepted traits of the psychic tableau. Where people may scoff about manipulation of subtle energy, or react dubiously towards someone claiming to be a telepath, most people accept the idea that someone is "an empath" at face value. I do not say "accept empathy" because it is natural that people would accept the sort of mundane meaning of empathy, the natural human tendency to commiserate and share in emotional experiences, as existent. Here I am talking about the psychic sense of empathy, the ability to feel deeply, as one's own, the emotions of others, *absent sensory information* that would otherwise clue one in. Empathy, like telepathy, is a form of *extrasensory perception*, or as it is sometimes called today, *anomalous cognition*.

Both of these skills can function absent any kind of energetic work, but the functioning of both tends to be reflected energetically and both can be emulated energetically. As we've previously discussed regarding imprinting, in many cases thoughts and emotions can be inadvertently imprinted onto objects or locations. Generally, stronger emotions or more intense thoughts will imprint themselves more strongly. Taking this a step further, however, we also know that people often maintain a constant chatter of mental and emotional activity. Because we all exist within a sort of substrate of subtle energy, and because of the interaction of the physical and mental worlds with the astral, or energetic world, our emotions and thoughts also imprint onto the ambient background with varying degrees of strength.

Consider dropping a pebble into a pool of water, then compare this to throwing the same pebble, or dropping a large rock. In each of these cases the water will behave slightly differently, with larger or more forceful stones causing a greater amount of disruption. Likewise, thoughts and feelings impact and are reflected energetically to different degrees depending on their gravity, the intensity at which they are thought or felt, and so on. Some people are naturally mentally louder and more forceful than others, and their mental and emotional activity is easier to detect. Similarly, some people are naturally more sensitive to this kind of psychic influence, and so respond to the energetic impressions of thought or the telepathic signals themselves.

You might also consider it something like a radio station, where multiple stations in the same area on the same frequency will overpower one another, but some signals are more powerful than others. Like a radio, too, the act of telepathic reception is passive, rather than active. The information is out there, and we must allow ourselves to receive it rather than try to go get it.

How do we allow ourselves to receive it? The first step returns to mental discipline. Looking back at the radio analogy, we have to consider that we are ourselves a broadcast tower of this emotional and mental activity. If we do not first turn down the power of our own broadcasts, we will have a much more difficult time of receiving other people's signals. Resting in a meditative state and quieting our own mind makes the process much easier. The next step is to attend to thoughts and ideas that arise and notice where they are coming from. Thoughts and emotions come and go with great frequency, and we tend to assume they are all ours. Because our "station" is very active, they likely *are* ours. However, if we are sitting quietly and our mind is also quiet, we may be able to notice that the thoughts and emotions of others are there and available. Like with subtle energy itself, because we are used to ignoring this kind of sensory modality, it can take practice before we start noticing the thoughts or emotions of others. They may seem foreign, but they may also seem a great deal like our own. It is this reason that natural telepaths and empaths often have some difficulty dealing with others, as it is difficult to differentiate their thoughts and feelings from those of other people.

We may also have to very mindfully and attentively "go looking" for other people's emotional states, but it is critical that this remain a passive process similar to listening carefully for a source of a noise or squinting to look more closely if something is available. This is not an active process of investigation or searching, as doing this is likely to heighten our own emotional and mental activity and thus undermine our goal of quieting the mind enough to "hear" the thoughts of others.

Regarding the nature of the thoughts we receive, it is rarely the case that we will achieve some kind of exact stream of consciousness from the people around us. While it is possible to achieve telepathic links with this degree of accuracy, it usually comes from a great deal of familiarity. Instead, it is much more common to receive a kind of pre-verbal mental impression from others. We may not know exactly what *words* they are thinking, but the concepts they are thinking *about* will arise in our mind, and, if our meditative stability is good, it will arise as *they* are thinking about it, rather than generating our own thoughts about that topic. If someone is thinking about lunch, for example, it may happen that we start thinking about lunch as well. If we lack mental discipline, the new thoughts about lunch will be our own. While the prompt of "lunch" did come from someone else, we haven't learned anything useful from this because our own mind contacted the idea of "lunch" and took off with it, rather than resting and allowing us to see where the other person's thoughts would take them.

Similarly, with emotions, it is common to feel the emotion but without its context we may mistake these for our own emotional states. Because, psychologically, emotion works through a process of physical arousal and mentally attributed rationalizations for those states, we run the risk here of mentally attributing our own reasons why we might feel that way, rather than recognizing the emotions as belonging to someone else and remaining passive to observe in greater detail where these emotions go or see if we can find particulars.

Returning to the topic of subtle energy and its interactions with telepathy and empathy, all of these thoughts and emotions create impressions on energy. We already have enough experience with energy, then, to read the passive impressions on the energy of people immediately around or near to us. By entering our resting state and allowing ourselves to sense thoughts and feelings we can receive this information from those around us. But what of people at a distance? This is arguably more useful as we could always just ask someone how they feel or what they're thinking if we're in a room together. If the skill hasn't naturally arisen at this point through practice and experimentation, we may need to practice sensing energy at a distance, which will be discussed in greater detail in the chapter on astral projection. The short of it is, we need here to shift our energetic awareness to a remote vantage point.

Such a projection of one's own awareness to a remote location is not always advantageous, however, and isn't much to do with subtle energy working directly. We can, however, use constructs to get this information. The most direct method would be to use the same tendrils we've discussed before. Here, we want to use the tendril as a sort of energetic tin can telephone. Reaching with the tendril towards the individual we're interested in, allow the impressions to "vibrate" down the tendril back to our own field, assuming the patterns from that remote location and imprinting on the tendril and, thus, back towards us. This is the simplest kind of telepathic contact, and happens to also be one of the more effective. It can also be used as a method for telepathic contact other than passive receiving. Whether someone is using a tendril or not, telepathic contact often leaves energetic traces that form such a tendril automatically through imprinting.

Just as we are able to passively receive telepathic information, others are as well, and this can be used to communicate the other way. Sending information can also be done along the tendril. As we think towards the other person, impressing our thoughts and feelings along the tendril, it can affect the other person's field as well and they may passively pick up on this. This alone may not be sufficient to send thoughts or ideas to an unwilling or unaware participant, however. Their own thoughts will likely be self-sustaining and so they will not be sensitive to the external imprints unless they are a natural telepath or waiting for the signal.

On the subject of telepathic sending, often called *projective telepathy*, it would be an error for me not to mention *pulse sending*. During the Cold War, significant research was conducted in telepathy as well as other psychic disciplines by both the United States and Soviet Union. At one point, research was being conducted to determine whether telepathy could be used to communicate with submarines under arctic pack ice, where radio could not penetrate. In an effort to determine the most reliable, effective way to send telepathically, many different methods were attempted. The best method by far ended up being to send thoughts towards a willing and ready recipient by thinking them in pulses. Rather than attempting to sustain attention on a single concept or idea steadily, thinking repeatedly towards the ready individual proved much better. If for example we're attempting to send the idea of a blue cube, it is better to think repeatedly "blue cube" in pulses than to try to just hold this idea while thinking at someone. Generally, the sender will time the pulses to something like the heartbeat or the second hand of a ticking clock. Meanwhile, the receiver enters the passive, receptive telepathic state as we have discussed earlier in this chapter. The simple message, sent again and again, spontaneously arises in the mind of the recipient, who writes down any impressions that arise during the time.

These impressions can then be compared to pre-arranged codebooks which contain more detailed instruction.

Obviously, for our purposes here, code books are not necessary. Instead, we can just send the shapes and colors, which is one of the more popular methods for practicing telepathic communication. Shapes and colors employ spatial and visual information and yet are intuitive abstractions that do not leave much room for interpretation, and therefore can easily be determined to be either hits or misses. This kind of practice is best for developing the skill as it allows us to differentiate the intended actual signal from the noise of our guessing or attempting to predict the answer. By carefully observing our own thoughts and receiving feedback on our responses we can learn to differentiate between our own mental fabrications and legitimate telepathic or energetic signals. It should be noted that this is not meant to be done as a way of grading someone's aptitude, but rather as a training tool for encouraging recognition of good information. It is often best to respond with "correct" on hits and to simply ignore misses, allowing a person to recognize the good information and simply filter out or ignore the bad, rather than calling attention to misses, as these are a natural occurrence especially in the early stages of training.

Pulse sending can be performed either by the direct telepathic method of "thinking at" a person, a process that is difficult to describe but something that we can rather intuitively understand, or by use of the tendril. Reaching out with the tendril and having it firmly connect on the other end to the other person's own energetic field, we can imprint the information we wish to communicate and then "send" it in pulses along the energetic link. This may be facilitated by visualizing the information traveling as a pulse down the tendril and imprinting itself on the other person's energetic field and mind. When we visualize it like this, however, it is best to only do so long enough to establish firmly what it is you're intending to do, and then bring your focus entirely to the information you're trying to send. Smaller, more distinctive messages incorporating multiple sensory modalities and greater detail are more likely to communicate, whereas, as with imprinting generally, vague and unclear concepts will communicate vague and unclear results.

This same approach applies when working with spirits and energetic beings in other planes. While most spirits do communicate telepathically, and most will "do the work" to bring a person up to their own communicative level temporarily, it is much easier to communicate firmly when keeping things both simple and non-verbal, rather than bogging it down with descriptive elaborations and words.

In addition to passively observing what someone is thinking about right now, we may be interested in what they think about certain topics specifically. We can query information telepathically by projecting a prompt which induces a person to think about a certain subject, and then projecting energy that amplifies the "reaction" to that projected prompt. It should be noted of course that this process is not particularly subtle, and a person with any kind of training is likely to notice what is happening. Even people without any kind of training will often physically sense this kind of energetic contact.

After establishing energetic links, as with working with any kind of energetic construct, it is good form for us to ground, center, and thoroughly dissolve these links. This is particularly true when working with telepathy as we can't really be sure what might come down the energetic line. While we have some limited control over our immediate area and while we can attentively regulate thoughts or feelings being communicated telepathically when we are attending to them, after we have finished practice or working we are likely to stop paying attention to whatever psychic information is coming along. However, we know that we do not need to be paying attention for something to be influential telepathically or empathically.

Open psychic connections can cause us unnecessary trouble, and it's best to ensure they are dissolved before we move on with our day. We should then ground and center, taking particular care to dump any impressions, programming, thoughts, or feelings that do not come from us.

ASTRAL PROJECTION

Previously we talked about communication through the imprinting of subtle energy, but had some difficulty in sensing energy over far distances without the use of a tendril or energetic link. This setback can be overcome through astral projection, though it is important that we not consider our ability to project the consciousness to be limited to the astral or energetic plane. It is certainly just as possible to project our consciousness through the material realm. When we project to other planes this is generally known as astral projection, but the same process done in the material plane is called having an out of body experience. Both of these are generally achieved the same way, with some people finding one easier than the other. I would generally say projection to the astral is easier, but only because we have fewer expectations of the sensory gestalt while Elsewhere. We have a sense for what we should experience in the material realm and in the absence of these sensory modes we tend to ignore them or dismiss them, or to sell ourselves short on the quality of our projection.

In any case, before discussing actual astral projection, I think it's prudent to discuss in slightly more detail what the astral is, why we would want to go there, and what kinds of things can be encountered there.

To begin, the astral planes exist as the interstitial space contacting the physical, mental, and etheric planes of existence in a model employed by the Western Hermetic philosophy. It reflects those planes while maintaining its own identity. It is an amalgamated plane of existence, the meta-plane which reflects and corresponds to all other planes. It is a bridge between the physical, etheric, and mental planes and so serves as a gateway. More directly, however, as it corresponds to all of these planes, it can be used to work in all of these planes. Work conducted in the astral reflects back to the other planes, and work conducted in other planes is reflected there as well. For this reason, astral projection has long been considered an important tool of the sorcerer, psychic, or magus.

We learn to project to the astral primarily as a means of interfacing with and magnifying effects remotely. The astral is generally more pliable, easier to shape and program and structure through thought, intention, and mental effort than the physical world. Where the application of mind over matter in the physical can result in some telekinetic effects, probability alterations, or so on, the astral responds as readily as subtle energy itself and then corresponds the work down to the physical plane. It's therefore possible to work much more elaborate designs astrally, and to more easily impact things in the physical world, without the need to actually travel to those places (although such travel can help). Essentially, one can perform greater workings for more magnificent results in the physical plane, albeit at a much slower pace. Besides this, such macro-psychokinetic effects are often beyond our grasp, while astral work is managed more often and more successfully.

Another reason for practicing astral projection is that many spirits and beings with energetic or etheric bodies can be contacted there directly, without necessarily summoning them directly to your own space. By working through the astral we can project a form into the etheric plane and interact with spirits in their own domain. While spirits can exist and influence the physical, and certainly can influence and exist in our own mental domains, the astral is the home to the forms of spirits such as deities, demigods, nagas, angels, and the like. While it is possible to contact these spirits without projection to the astral, through ritual, divination, or so on, contact in the astral can provide a more visceral sensory experience of spirit contact. This kind of contact can be informative and useful in a variety of ways generally beyond the scope of this book. It should be noted, however, that while the astral maintains some characteristics of the physical, experiences of the astral are often hallucinatory and dream-like, and so projectors seeking to simply inhabit another body like through virtual reality are likely to be disappointed.

As for more local out of body experiences, these can be used for some limited forms of remote viewing, as well as for the remote sensing of energy. Projecting the consciousness other places on the physical plane can give us information about the energy in that area as our consciousness interacts with this subtle energy directly rather than through the sensory modalities of our physical body. While we may prefer to use sensory overlays as discussed before for perceiving energy, the actual sensation of energy seems to work through contact with the consciousness. By sending our consciousness elsewhere we can gather information about and manipulate energy remotely, and also pursue limited clairvoyant applications, using the energetic impressions and imprints to paint a conceptual picture of the location.

To actually engage in the practice of astral projection it is helpful to first have a solid foundational understanding that the consciousness, while linked causally to the physical body, is not anywhere to be found or dependent on the body. We often wish to associate the consciousness with the function of the brain, but the brain can be understood more to be co-emergent with, rather than causal of, the conscious mind. Each influences the other, but they arise through shared causes and conditions, reflecting as above, so below. When we project astrally, we send the consciousness out of our physical body to somewhere else. Doing so does not separate the function of the brain from the function of the consciousness, because their physical distance or planar proximity is unimportant except inasmuch as the physical brain, as the physical interface for physical sensation causes this sensory information to arise in the consciousness as perceptions. At the very least, it supports the arising of this information and anchors our consciousness in physical senses. In effect, it is a limiting factor on our consciousness, serving as a filter of information that through strongly formed habit we rely on rather than other information to which we have access but do not perceive through the physical sense organs, such as information about energy, others' thoughts and feelings, the dispositions of other beings, and the like.

The goal here is to move the consciousness outside the body while perceiving the information and senses of our consciousness itself rather than the physical senses. A successful astral projection can be very disorienting for people the first time, because the conventional physical senses which we are used to are not useful here and in fact can be a hindrance. Finding our consciousness in strange and unfamiliar places, we look through habit to our old modes of sensory investigation and find that the physical senses on which we usually rely do not seem to reflect the place we find ourselves. It can take many successful projections before we achieve anything other than disorientation and withdrawing back to the body's familiar senses.

There are many approaches towards astral projection. I prefer to first induce an out of body experience. This gets us familiar first with leaving the physical body and then turning this into a successful astral projection is more an issue of managing the destination than of getting out of body.

Starting from the meditative, resting state, sit comfortably in a reclining chair, or lie down. There is naturally a significant risk of falling asleep here, but if we fall asleep little harm is done. If we are standing or sitting upright we run the risk of falling over from disorientation, which could be if nothing else harmful to our pride, but potentially much worse. Better to get comfortable in such a way that the body is fully supported. Ideally, lie down somewhere where the whole body is supported and comfortable. Stretch and relax from your toes up to the top of your head, progressively flexing and relaxing each muscle until you are receiving minimal physical sensation.

Limit light and sound as distracting sensory information can creating an irritating anchor for the consciousness to fixate on.

Thus relaxed, visualize your own body as completely comprised of and full of energy, as we already have done. Visualize your consciousness as existing within this energetic body, which exists in the same space as your own physical body. Firmly anchor and establish that your consciousness is present there. Now, without moving your physical arm, reach up ahead of you with your energetic arm. Fully recognize your energetic arm and body to respond reflexively to the mental commands of your consciousness just as your physical body effortlessly responds to your thoughts and directions. Move your arm about, feeling it move without physically moving it. Repeat this with your other arm. Sit your legs up. Do all this without physically moving.

Now, we can attempt several different visualizations, but the goal is to have this energetic body stand or float up and away from your physical body. With this energetic body in which our consciousness abides, simply roll over or sit up out of the physical body, standing or floating up until the energetic body is physically removed. At this point, we should try opening our visualized energetic eyes, taking a "look" at our physical body there. This will help with our consciousness, our mind, recognizing which senses it should be attending to. If we are looking at our own body from another perspective, we can see that the physical body is not the basis of all perception and this will help us cultivate other sensation while projected out of body.

Alternatively, one might visualize themselves as floating up and out of the physical body, or falling backwards and out of the physical body. The visualization itself is not important so long as the energetic body is responding directly to the consciousness just as if we were moving our own physical body, but without moving the physical body. As I type this, I do not think about each finger and hand moving about the keyboard directing each action consciously, rather, I just think about what I'm trying to type, and the body just does it automatically. We should ideally have the same kind of control over the energetic body.

While I've used the idea of an energetic form or body here, this also does not need to be the case. As mentioned before, the consciousness is an aggregation of phenomena, and does not exist in a place. Because of this, it need not be "located" anywhere, and the awareness can move about the astral without any kind of representative energetic form. Thinking this way works better for some people who need to shed the concept of the physical body more thoroughly to succeed in exiting the body. Later, with practice, we can project the consciousness itself to physical places or to the astral, etheric, or mental planes without any effort and without having to establish a supportive energetic form. However, this is a more advanced application that requires some familiarity and the ability to quickly leave the body. For now, it is best that we practice with a supportive etheric form. This can also serve to help orient us spatially Elsewhere[18], and to ground or anchor us to some support for our consciousness until we are more familiar with the kind of raw information we receive astrally without conventional sensation or perception.

No matter the approach one chooses to take here, the first astral projection can take some time to achieve. Diligent practice for at least an hour or so per day should yield results in a few weeks. It is important to try one thing multiple times without changing the scheme too much. If we try different visualizations and approaches each day, we are unlikely to succeed with any of them. As long as the visualization and

---

[18] Here "Elsewhere" refers to any place that is projected to, generally in the astral or mental planes. The term is contrasted glibly with the "really-real world," referring to consensus material reality.

concepts make sense, an approach can work. If after two or three weeks no signs of progress are seen, then you should consider changing the approach. Some signs of progress are dizziness and disorientation, a feeling like a pulsing, buzzing, or vibrating through the whole body, or a stretching or pulling sensation like gravity exists above and below at the same time. For many people, when these sensations appear, it creates a final hurdle to proper projection. The sensation is so sudden and violent that it instantly pulls the consciousness back into the body, due to our strong habituation towards physical senses. It takes practice and perseverance, as well as strong meditative stability, to bypass this, but when we do so success is in our hands.

The first time many people project this energetic form away from the body they do not usually get very far. The bizarreness of the experience can be disorienting even to those who are very well prepared for it. A common experience is falling rapidly back into the body, often accompanied with the sensation of falling or hitting the surface we're resting on, as if we'd struck the ground in a dream. These kinds of experiences should be encouraging rather than discouraging as they serve as an evident transitional state demonstrating a successful projection. While they are not the *goal*, they are a good sign. As you become more successful moving out of the body, you will be able to more easily tell when a projection has been successful and work to orient yourself.

To return to the body, move the etheric body to lay back down such that it overlays the physical again, and transition the consciousness back. Alternatively, return the consciousness on its own, or simply transition your focus back to a physical sense to anchor. Even if the physical body has fallen asleep, we can focus on the feeling of our breath. When we attempt to focus on this, the consciousness will shift back to the physical body in order to make use of physical senses. If after you shift your consciousness back to the body you find yourself paralyzed, do not worry. Like when we sleep, the physical body sometimes paralyzes itself when we project in order to prevent us from acting out on erroneous impulses while the brain is left to manage things on its own.

Returning to the body can also be disorienting and it's not uncommon for an astral projector to be somewhat uncoordinated and dazed for some time following projection. This can result from the consciousness remaining somewhat split between the projected location and the physical body's senses. Remote viewers refer to this as "bilocation." It is inadvisable to drive, operate machinery, or so on in such a state. Another common occurrence is what we might call a "hard landing," slamming forcefully back into the physical body and senses with a start. As before, this can only serve as confirmation of a successful projection.

With practice, the consciousness can be projected, or *reached*, to another location without going through the steps of pacifying the physical body and limiting sensory input. Some routine astral projectors end up splitting their conscious awareness between the really real world and the astral Elsewhere so deftly that they are never fully present in one or the other. While this can be useful to some spirit workers and so on, I would suggest against it unless the benefits outweigh the loss of concentration and awareness of one's surroundings that can result.

To project to the astral, we repeat the same steps and processes as before, but this time with the firm intention of travelling astrally. To this end, project the etheric body as before. The next bit is perhaps a little difficult to explain, but I will do my best. Once you are out of the physical body and fully in the etheric body, choose an empty space in front of yourself and step through that space into the space between. You might consider using the hand like a knife to cut the air in front of you, then step through this, or pull it apart with both hands. In either case this is more of a conceptual tool to help one conceive of the astral for the first time when they have never been. Other techniques can include stepping through mirrors, or creating gates or doors. These techniques can be performed ritually for those inclined towards ceremonial magic, but such methods vary dramatically across traditions. In any case practitioners of religious or magical traditions that include astral projection should not be doing so anyhow until instructed with the methods of that lineage out of courtesy and respect to the system. If you have friends who have successfully projected, you can ask them to lay a "beacon" or signal line down which you can travel, as well.

As with our first out of body experience, the astral itself can be extremely disorienting. While in the physical world the sensory modalities we are used to continue to work. In the astral it takes considerable skill with sensory overlays to achieve anything resembling a successful mapping of this new energetic-information oriented awareness to a mode we're used to. If there is any kind of visceral sensory experience, it is likely to be dreamlike and bizarre. For many people, the experience tends to be described as simply "knowing" what is going on, and that is in fact a success. Many people are discouraged when they project and do not have the feelings of physical presence, with full perception in the sensory modalities we are used to physically. This should not be discouraging. Rather, it should be the opposite. It's unreasonable to think that we would have the same form of sensory perception in a completely different plane of reality as we do in this one, where such sensory perception is based on an aggregation of causes and conditions. Elsewhere, too, consists of such causes and conditions, but the sensation of it is very different. Indeed, "just knowing" what is going on can be abstractly remapped to sensory channels. Care must be taken, however, because the astral is much more responsive to our thoughts. Attempts to visualize what is there must be made with care, as we can easily manifest what we expect to be there into actually being there, resulting in a kind of chicken and egg scenario where we attempt to create a visual sensory overlay but in so doing also create the thing we are trying to perceive, which we then try to see visually, reinforcing it. Fortunately, we can usually dissolve anything that is created through flippancy or poor mental discipline as easily as we inadvertently created it.

Perhaps more commonly than with people's first experiences working with energy, many people encounter a wide variety of spirits and entities shortly after their first projections astrally. The act of astral projection seems to identify one as a possible contact for spirits and sentient beings that exist energetically in our local physical world. There are a great number of spirits that coexist with us in the physical realm but with whom we usually do not interact directly as they are imperceptible to our physical senses. However, the overlap of the etheric and physical planes in the astral demonstrates a possibility for them to communicate with us in the neutral ground of the astral. In this day and age where we are all much more preoccupied with only the physical world, it is much less common for spirits to encounter people who will communicate back with them when they attempt communication. An astral projector, then, who can travel to them and communicate with them on their "own ground," so to speak, is therefore naturally very interesting to many spirits, and it is common for new projectors to find themselves experiencing attempts at contact from spirits in both the astral and physical world.

How you react to this is up to you, but I generally suggest a peaceful, friendly approach, either seeing what the spirits want, or making them some small offerings and asking that they leave you alone. The traditional approach of heavy-handed banishing is usually unnecessarily forceful and the habit of using a confrontational approach can cause trouble in future work with spirits. You can also use shielding and warding around the areas both from whence and to which one projects, hiding oneself or making things seem boring or uninteresting. Creating a shield into which spirits cannot enter may help for avoiding contacts in the home, and so on. Still, these approaches rely on spirits only attempting to make contact immediately during or after the projection and in the same place astrally, whereas some live in the same physical places as we do, and so will simply wait. Essentially, it is sometimes better to answer the phone call and let the caller know you don't want to talk, than to ignore it and let the phone ring and ring, lest they just wait and call back later.

As for application, once astral travel has been successfully achieved, and we have some kind of stability there, the same techniques for making constructs, imprinting energy, and so on can be achieved and in the same ways. Additionally, the skill of projecting the consciousness lets us reach across vast distances to sense the energy in areas away from us. This obviously has applications for communication, as was discussed previously. It is also another method by which we can work remotely, without necessarily sending long tendrils of energy over great physical distances from our own physical body. It becomes much easier to project our consciousness to the remote location and do the work as if we were present there. In this case, we would use another source of energy for our work, one closer to the targeted location, rather than drawing it off our own bodies.

The potential to create and store constructs and objects and to work with pocket-spaces - private dimensions that do not correspond to anywhere physical but only to our own mental plane - in the astral is great, but for now it more is important to practice the skill of projecting the consciousness, working there to a limited degree, and returning successfully. It should be noted here also that returning to the physical body remains the default state so long as the physical body continues functioning. Many people concern themselves about "getting stuck" projected, but, in my experience, this never happens. Instead, the physical body falls asleep, and forcefully pulls a person back upon waking. This is yet another reason for developing meditative stability, so that the physical body does not fall asleep and interfere in longer work or begin interjecting in what we're doing with dreams.

Practicing the projection of consciousness builds the foundation for most long-distance work and scanning, and gives us the toolset to begin working in the astral. It is important to first learn to concentrate, as the astral's responsiveness to our thoughts makes it potentially troublesome for our mind to wander. The potential for manifesting our own fears, concerns, neuroses, and so on is tremendously magnified with successful projection. If you have been cultivating a stable mind, however, this is unlikely to be a great risk or of any real concern. Still, after the first visits to the astral for the purpose of experimentation and learning, it is best to limit projection to times when there is a goal in mind to be achieved, as we can all have strange thoughts which arise and which can be made manifest through projection into the astral. Even individuals who spend much or all of their time partially projected to the astral learn quickly to shift their awareness off of the astral consciousness so as not to inadvertently manifest any random thought or emotion.

Like with energetic constructs, thoughts, emotions, feelings, concepts and so on can also be manifested much more plainly and simply on the astral. This can be used to amplify or magnify the effect of our physical-plane energetic constructs. As mentioned before, effects can be enhanced by recruiting and working on multiple levels at once. If we, for example, have a physical object with some kind of symbolic power (an engraving, or an object sympathetic to the desired effect), which we then ward with the thing we wish to imprint on it, and then which we link to the same effect astrally, while strongly forming the intention both astrally and in the physical energetic work, we can improve the likelihood of success and amplify the influence of the work. The more vectors we use to approach something, here, the better.

After projection it is even more important to thoroughly ground and center as this will help to refocus and reestablish the consciousness in the physical body. Rattling and cleaning one's field may also be warranted depending on what kinds of activities or places one has projected to. The centering and grounding process to anchor the consciousness back in the physical body is not only healthy in this case for the energetic form but also can help with symptoms of bilocation and with the occasional problem of spontaneously and unintentionally projecting the consciousness.

I would also suggest against making projection into a cantrip. Use of ritual can be very effective at ensuring that projection is achieved successfully and reliably, but the multiple steps ritual generally takes serves as a safeguard against spontaneous accidental projection, which can be both disorienting and dangerous if it happens at a wrong or inconvenient time. It is always good to make sure that projection should be intentional and deliberate and should require at the very least a conscious decision to project and where to project. Setting cantrips creates the risk of inadvertently projecting without preparation or forethought.

CLAIRVOYANCE

One of the more admired personalities within psychicism generally is that of the clairvoyant, the psychic who can see clearly. Generally, clairvoyance is something of a misnomer. While it means "clear sight," such sight is rarely ever clear, but rather comes as series of informational impressions. When coupled with a rigorous protocol and using a series of controls, it is termed Remote Viewing, and is a subject for an entirely separate book. Like telepathy, clairvoyance is not always related to energy working. The clairvoyant may receive information directly, the signal spontaneously arising mentally. However, if we have developed a sensitivity to energy or the ability to project astrally, it is possible to receive similar information through these mechanisms, and most clairvoyants who have trained to acquire the skill do so through sensitivity to energetic or astral imprinting, sometimes, but not always, using a visual sensory overlay to produce this kind of "seeing."

The information that is associated with energy from objects, thoughts, and so on is not always what we consider pure "thought" information, such as emotions or ideas, but also perceptual information. The idea that a gold ring is made out of gold and is gold in color is all information about it. Any thought that might arise from contact with an object is information about the object that is echoed energetically and astrally. Perception, after all, is the mental recognition and idea-formation about a thing based on the sensory input our organs receive. Without the sensory organ in play, there remains this kind of ascribed information. The more commonly an object has been interacted with by sentient beings, who reinforce and strengthen the imprinting process, the less abstract the informational imprinting will be, and the more strongly accessible it will be.

We can accomplish this kind of clairvoyance either through the use of energetic links, or through astral projection. In the former the process is not so different from the one used in telepathic applications. Having performed all of the basic preliminaries, reach out with an energetic tendril to contact the object. Importantly, one does not need to know where the object is, and this is in fact one of the basic applications of clairvoyance: finding objects. If you can visualize the object, you can reach out to it mentally with these links and then, quieting the mind, allow yourself to sense the information about its location, or if you are searching for an object nearby, follow the link like reeling yourself on a fishing line.

One does not need to know what the object is, or anything else about it, either. Instead, you can use the information *about* it, that it is the thing being sought after, to reach your link towards *that*. If a person asks you to find an object, it is enough to energetically reach towards "the object" and then quietly sense the energy accordingly. The reason this is hypothesized to work is because "the object is being sought" becomes associated information which imprints informationally on the object. While this is not strictly an energetic imprinting, that pure information about it is hypothesized to become part of what has been termed a conceptual matrix of information which can be used to index objects and information about essentially anything. It is this informational matrix by which remote viewing has also been speculated to work. In this case, anyhow, we are only using that raw information to which we already have access to give us a target for the direction of energy. From that point, we can sense the imprinted information from the energy as usual.

It's also possible to clairvoyantly sense a *location* by similar means, reaching out to a place and then receiving the radiating informational imprints from objects at the location. For training purposes, it is ideal not to know what the location is, and for the location to have been assigned by another person such that it can be verified for accuracy as the information is sensed. As when we practiced sensing energetic imprints before, the training process is one of differentiating accurate signal information from inaccurate noise or mental fabrication resultant from knowing too much about the object beforehand.

The alternative approach is through astral projection. As the astral reflects the physical world, it is possible to project our consciousness to an astral location correspondent to a physical location. When we do so, the strong energetic imprints that are found can reflect the physical reality. However, in this case it can be difficult to determine if what we sense astrally is exactly accurate. Energetic imprints and reflections in the astral can be delayed as the development of new energetic patterns take some time and reinforcement to propagate, such as in the case of new construction or repurposing of land. A forest that has been paved through to make a road may still astrally reflect a forest for some time. The trees may have been cleared away, but unless some deliberate effort is made, the energetic imprint of those trees can remain for a very long time. Similarly, when new structures are built, they may not be imprinted strongly at first. Notable exceptions to this tend to be religious sites, as the ritual consecration of these places tends to energetically charge them such that they are reflected very strongly in the astral. Locations that have been the sites of pilgrimages or other focus points such as battlefields, prisons, or so on often also strongly imprint astrally, and this can persist for quite a long time, just as their energetic impressions that we can sense without astral projection can be quite strong.

This kind of projection to a location for the astral correspondence can be tricky, and often requires a degree of sensitivity to find smaller or less significant objects. Often, these become something of a blur. If we were to describe the astral sense in the terms of vision, or using an overlay, we could say that objects of acute interest or strong energetic imprints can be seen sharply and clearly, while objects with small imprints or little significance become blurry and fade into the background imagery. As with normal vision, if we're looking for something particular it is possible to squint and make out the finer details from the blurriness, and so we can specifically look at certain objects.

It is also possible to query objects by establishing both energetic links in the material realm or via the astral. To do this, once the link is established, send energy along it with the intention of imprinting with the desired information. If we are trying to determine the color of an object, for example, we can send energy toward the object with the intention of imprinting the energy with the object's color. We can then sense the newly flared energy in the normal way. Astrally, we can do the exact same thing, sending energy into the astral form of the object and imprinting it with the information that we're looking for from that object. In either case it is important to frame the intention with some nuance, being sure that we're imprinting the actual information about the object by magnifying the information already imprinted on the energetic reflection, rather than by trying to guess the object's color, shape, or whatever we're looking for and then imprinting that. The latter will essentially cast a rather weak spell to change the object's color.

As always, we should finish any kind of clairvoyant sensing session by dumping information through grounding and centering. It is also important to do this between targets, as it will minimize, though not eliminate, the possibility of information from one target being maintained in our mind and erroneously ascribed to the next target. This kind of grounding and centering by this point should be habitual and nearly automatic, but it remains critically important.

Practicing clairvoyance can be done many ways. It is easiest done with a partner, who can hide or assign objects or places to serve as targets as well as provide feedback during a practice session to help one differentiate signal from noise. It is important in this kind of practice to safeguard against two things. The first and most obvious problem would be that the partner coaches or overprovides information. This could lead us to false positives, which would not help us differentiate signal from noise but instead would only get us very good at reading body language. It is better, then, that the partner not always have access to the information but rather that the whole session be done via a double blind; that is, having the friend's *friend* hide it. The other concern when working with a partner who knows what the target is, is that we would employ the wrong kind of psychic faculty and *telepathically* gather this information. While this is still an impressive psychic feat, it is not what we're trying to learn or develop.

It is also possible to practice clairvoyance without a partner, either by viewing a location that is being recorded and comparing impressions to the recordings later, or by use of randomized target cards. The latter is done by assigning targets ahead of time, writing them on cards and placing these cards into envelopes. The envelopes are then shuffled, and the clairvoyance is attempted on "the target written on the card inside this envelope." A similar method is sometimes employed by remote viewers who practice at home, although the method of clairvoyance we've outlined here is very different from remote viewing, in that it lacks protocol and functions somewhat differently. In any case, once the cards are assigned and shuffled in envelopes, we can practice without a partner by viewing those things we've written down. We can also use targets assigned from remote viewing practice pools, easily found online. While we are not doing remote viewing in this case, the target assignment system can be the same. Know that remote viewers typically use coordinates, and so our prompt here would be "the target referred to by the coordinates . . . "

Like with any of these psychic senses, improvement comes with regular practice, so establishing a system to practice clairvoyance daily is best. The faculty may also improve through the training of unrelated things like remote sensing of energy or remote viewing. Remote viewing in particular is a protocol driven method for clairvoyance which is excellent for gathering information about targets, although the term "viewing" is something of a misnomer as the visual sense channel is not the only or even main sensory format used. In any case, remote viewing would exceed the scope of this book, but because of the rigorous study that has gone into it through its development by various intelligence agencies, an abundance of information on the subject is easily available.

WORKING WITH SPIRITS

It is necessary to discuss the topic of working with spirits as it invariably comes up. There is significant discussion as to the nature of spirits, where they come from, how they behave, and so on, but that is not a topic for this book. Nevertheless, spirits, as sentient beings with consciousness, are able to influence and be influenced by subtle energy just as we are. And, unlike us, they lack physical form and so are to some extent *more* easily influenced than we are.

Regardless of the spirit, we can interact with them essentially in the same way we would interact with anyone through the use of subtle energy. Anyone telepathy, empathic, or clairvoyant effect that can influence a person can influence a spirit. And person sensitive to the telepathic, empathic, or energetic influence of people or places will be similarly sensitive to those same influences by spirits. In some circles, these individuals can be of particular use. For example, in paranormal investigation, energetically sensitive individuals can often serve as inducers, if not as mediums.

There is particular value to working with subtle energy in paranormal investigation as well as in exorcisms, evocations, or any workings where spirits are involved.

Paranormal investigation is one of the more obvious applications, but the ins and outs of this relationship can be complicated. One question I am frequently asked is whether energy can be detected with paranormal investigation instruments, if subtle energy is the same "stuff" that spirits work with. It's not an unreasonable question, but it lacks an understanding of paranormal investigation tools and methods.

Paranormal investigators use a number of different tools in order to investigate sites, individuals, situations and so on to determine if there is empirical evidence that is anomalous. There is no technology that can actually detect spirits. Indeed, even at haunted locations, if a spirit does not wish to be found the paranormal investigator's tools will be useless. Instead, these tools are designed to document either environmental anomalies that might indicate something paranormal is present, or to allow spirits a medium for communication that isn't dependent on an individual.

The first sets of tools are what we most commonly associate with paranormal investigation. These are the electromagnetic field (EMF) detectors, electronic voice phenomena (EVP) recorders, Geiger counters to detect radiation, special cameras with a variety of ranges and options, and so on. More recently, other tools have been developed as digital mediums, allowing the spirit to communicate by, for example, influencing the outputs of a random number generator using micro-PK like influences.

Subtle energy can affect and impact these things, but they do not directly detect subtle energy in and of themselves. Thus it is *possible* that our own energy work can be detected by these devices, but only if what we're doing has an impact in the real empirical reality these devices detect. Not all spirits will be located by an EMF detector, not all spirits choose to interact with an EVP recorder. Neither of these will necessarily detect our own subtle energy work, but with practice and skill they can be used to react. Some years ago, for example, I met a gentleman who was able to influence a Geiger counter by directing energy at it; but this does not demonstrate that subtle energy is radioactive! I believe a similar effect could be achieved through practicing with, for example, an EMF detector.

The second category of devices, the digital mediums, serve the same purpose as an actual medium. Generally, mediums are individuals who, through some psychic faculty, can communicate with and on behalf of spirits. A telepathic medium will receive direction from a spirit (called the control), who can relay whatever messages. The accuracy and detail of this communication is limited by a number of factors, including the telepath's sensitivity, the complication and clarity of the message itself, and, perhaps most commonly ignored, the spirit's own telepathic faculty. While spirits are generally capable of some limited telepathy, it is not always very clear and it is usually conducted much the same way as the telepathic method presented in the earlier chapter—interactions of subtle energy fields with imprinted information.

Thus subtle energy work can present an opportunity for communication in paranormal investigation. Notably, however, these communications are not in and of themselves valid empirical data for such an investigation. They do not meet the standards of evidence that reputable paranormal investigators hold themselves to, as they could be the result of delusion or fraud. That said, there's no reason these tools cannot be employed together. A telepathic medium can communicate more clearly with a spirit than speaking aloud, for example. As a result, a telepath could induce a spirit to interact with investigative tools that they would not have otherwise. Additionally, spirits tend to be interested in individuals with active, clean, vibrant energy fields that indicate they will be receptive to the spirit's own attempts at communication. The mere presence of an energy worker can be sufficient to induce paranormal phenomena.

Importantly, spirits are rarely actually deceased humans. Generally, hauntings fall into two categories: energetic imprints of individuals which have been sustained in the form of sophisticated energetic constructs, and sentient spirits which communicate with us for the same reasons we might be interested in communicating with them. These spirits are not the spirits of the deceased but merely beings like us, though with their own unique qualities and characteristics.

There are a number of basic energy working we'd want to consider when working with spirits. In fact, all of the skills covered in this book have some application. Effective detection of, communication with, and interaction with spirits are one of the primary reasons for energy work at all. However, unlike with astral projection we are going Elsewhere and interacting with spirits in some intangible and abstract not-place, here we are working with spirits within our own time and place.

When working with spirits it is important to remain grounded and centered. Our actual sensitivity to subtle energy itself is contingent largely upon the health and welfare of our own energetic body. Where it is dull and stagnant it is more difficult for the spirit's influences to be felt, and so we may not notice attempts at communication. Additionally, blocked or slowed energetic channels may not be as effective at directing subtle energy in attempts at influencing spirits.

Shields and fields can be used directly to either attract or repel spirits. Spirits are simply sentient beings like us, and like us they have different interests, likes, and dislikes. Often, the class of spirit can determine these, but not always. In the language of magic, characteristics or properties that attract spirits are called sympathetic, and those that repel spirits are called antipathetic. Just as before, we can attract spirits by programming fields that have properties they enjoy, and we can repel them with properties they dislike. This can be done with actual objects (as in ritual magic), but it can also be accomplished through the creation of constructs. After all, whereas we have a physical body which largely anchors our energetic form, spirits are entirely energetic forms, and so disruptive fields can be very harmful to them.

Shields can be created as barriers to hold spirits out (or in), and even when interacting with ritual magicians, witches, or so on the observant energy worker will notice the formation of meta-constructs resultant from the ritual. While sorcery is not itself merely a "form of energy work," the actions of sorcerers and so on are reflected in energetic forms just as physical actions are reflected energetically. Similarly, performing some kind of action energetically does not necessarily bring about the physical result, but it *can*.

Communication with spirits can be accomplished through the same energetic channels as has been introduced previously for telepathy and empathy. Acting as a medium through energy work is generally a fairly safe way of doing this. Rather than invoking the spirit into us and allowing them to control the body, we can simply relay messages on the spirit's behalf. This can be done without taking the spirit into one's energy field the same as it's accomplished when working with people: a tendril of energy can be sent to touch the spirit's field and information can be relayed through this tendril via energetic imprinting.

There are considerations when using this approach, however. For one, subtle energy is not a convenient medium for communicating specific phrases or words. As with normal telepathy, the message conveyed is generally a pre-conceptual proto-thought which we generate ourselves as a thought and so which can be flavored by our own preconceptions. It is important, then, to maintain a "blind" to the target spirit, so that we do not allow our own preconceptions to poison communication, if accurate communication is our goal. Similarly, when attempting to communicate back to the spirit through energetic means, keeping concepts simple is ideal. Yes and no, firm statements, and so on are often fairly easy to communicate through imprinting, but it would be difficult to imprint an entire speech or long list of ideas in a reliable way.

Essentially all of these applications are a form of psychometry. We detect the spirit itself through noticing its influence in the environment. It's possible for a spirit to be nearly impossible to find and locate spatially if it is capable of contracting the field considerably, or by withdrawing its field entirely from the spatial etheric field in the case of astral beings. As discovered previously, there is a near-astral which relates to the physical world around us in space and time, and a farther astral which does not. Because spirits have no corporeal form to serve as a tether, it is generally not difficult for them to choose to be in other places.

In some cases we may even want to use constructs to give spirits an "abode" to inhabit. Some spirits have such subtle fields that they cannot easily interact with even the ethereal plane, and so interaction with the physical world is nearly impossible. By creating a construct that a spirit can inhabit and take on as an ethereal form, present with us in space and time, we can allow communications from very subtle or distant spirits indeed. However, it should be noted these spirits are generally not the subject of paranormal investigation, as their subtle astral forms do not tend to attract the attention of people not looking for them.

However, this is not to be confused with the creation of "servitors" or "egregores," discussed in the next chapter. Here we are mainly creating an energetic vessel for a spirit to inhabit, where the consciousness and behavior comes from a pre-existing spirit and not one of our own design. Similar approaches can be accomplished in the physical world through the creation of "abodes" or "spirit houses" meant to serve as physical homes for spirits to inhabit, where they can receive offerings or be found and called upon.

Some spirits, based on their own likes and dislikes, will find abodes on their own, and finding these homes can be another use for psychometry. Often, spirits will attach themselves to objects of no particular significance; but when these objects are brought into a home they can become the cause of a haunting. In some cases, the easiest way to remediate a haunting can be to find the object of the spirit's sympathy and simply remove it from the home. If this is not acceptable, and peaceful communication cannot convince the spirit to leave on agreeable terms, then energy work can also be used to expel the spirit, through either the introduction of antipathetic energetic imprints or through depatterning or other energetic works harmful to spirits.

Care should be taken, however, that our own increased sensitivity to energy work does leave us somewhat more susceptible to the influence of spirits. Energetic effects imprint onto the physical world just the same, and so influences on our own energy body can cause physical illness. Negative or harmful probabilities through micro-PK like applications can lead to serious accidents or harm. Our physical forms are more vulnerable than we often like to admit, and the curse of a spirit can be very dangerous indeed. Working with spirits in hostile ways can lead to spirits working on us with the same hostility, and in these cases self-defense in the form of shields and fields becomes not just a good habit, but a necessity.

Spirits may also not distinguish between people who have caused them harm. Local land spirits rarely take the time to track down the person who disturbs their home, instead lashing out at whoever is nearby. These spirits can be particularly harmful as they have longstanding connections that vastly increase their ability to work with the natural world in ways people struggle much harder to achieve. Before we do any energetic workings that may be harmful to spirits, it's a good practice to communicate our intent ahead of time. It's also important to let people know when we're going to be doing energy working involving spirits they are around often. We may think we're doing someone a favor expelling a spirit from their home without their knowledge, but we may cause them considerable grief when that spirit comes back after we leave, having disrupted a previously harmonious coexistence.

For further reading on this topic, please see my other book, Subtle Spirits: A Handbook of Hauntings and Psychic Mediumship.

INTERFACING WITH MAGIC: THOUGHTFORMS AND SERVITORS

As mentioned before, working with subtle energy itself and directly can be very limiting. Taking this approach, we are automatically only working with energy to which we ourselves have access, and we often find ourselves working to crossed purposes with others or just trying to overcome the general static of the world. On its own, subtle energy work tends to remain encapsulated in its own domain, isolated from the general magical community and even somewhat from the psychic community as its own set of practices. This is ultimately very limiting, and energetic work tends to work best when paired with other things. We can however enhance or improve our use of traditional tools of magic, and vice versa, to improve the effectiveness of our workings.

The most basic tool of the magician is a set of symbolic associations which they use to bring about an effect they desire. Whether it is the stodgy ceremonial magician in Tau robes chanting incantations in Hebrew or Latin, or the modern chaos magician using memes and pop culture to evoke their unconscious desires, the use of activated symbolism is the basic language shared by magic. Paired with subtle energy working, we can activate our magical goals through a combined method that simultaneously acts via Hermetic correspondence as well as through mobilizing our will.

One very basic way to do this is through the use of advanced constructs which embody the magical results we're trying to bring about. For example, someone interested in the Kabbalah may build energetic constructs external or internal to him or herself which correspond to the Tree of Life. By meditation and focus on the construct as well as the direction of subtle energy towards it, we lend our own energy directly to fuel a magical process which is dictated in shorthand by the symbolic association. The more intimately we're familiar with the symbol set, and the more intuitively and deeply the symbols speak to us, the better they serve as shorthand for a magical goal. This pre-existing, culturally transmitted and encoded set of beliefs, understandings, or associations with a symbol or idea is called the *egregore*, and we can use this in energy work to quickly form complex constructs.

For this reason, gaining a working familiarity with magical symbols is useful even for the strict energy manipulator. We should also focus on working with the symbols that speak to us, taking care that symbols from foreign cultures be studied in great depth and within their cultural context. A symbol to some extent gains its power both from the strength of its meaning formed by its meaning and use by entire civilizations as well as from the depth that this shared tradition gives it to speak to members of that culture. While a person may have disdain for the religious practices of their own culture, for example, those symbols speak deeply and intuitively to us because of their hegemony. To discard the use of, for example, Christian symbolism and meaning entirely in favor of symbols from another culture is to weaken the magician's own power to tap those deeply held mental ideas, and to substitute superficially learned symbols that do not have the same emotional and, thus, magical impact.

That's not to say that use of other foreign symbols is impossible or will necessarily be weaker; however, if we don't take care to study a symbol or idea very completely any working we attempt to undertake will be incomplete. Without a full cultural context for an idea, without a deep understanding of its place as part of an interconnected whole, the application of a symbol will not work as well. Symbols work as a magical shorthand and in this use work as a tool for energetic focus because they bring with them a rich and complete network of interconnectedness which serves as a shorthand for an operation. Absent this strong tradition, we may as well make use of our own fabricated symbols and avoid the potentially unintended consequences of working with ideas and meanings we don't fully understand.

This, too, is very popular and common. The creation of a *sigil* in the modern sense is little more than the development of a representative glyph or icon which represents a ritual or spell of our own creation. Historically, sigils were often created using systems as part of a consistent whole within a tradition. For example, planetary sigils use magic squares related to the different planetary powers and intelligences in order to all on that power to enact the sorcerer's goals. Today, such symbols do not always correspond to a magic square, and may instead be created by one's own methods, so long as they somehow encode a meaning that speaks deeply to the caster of the sigil. Sigils, being products of the creativity of the energy worker, and carrying a fully formed meaning association created by the caster, can be formed into energetic constructs as well and then placed as wards or charged as functional constructs. Such a construct, being charged and imprinted with a symbol that carries out a specific task, is called a *thoughtform*.

The term "thoughtform" was perhaps first used by William Walker Atkinson to refer to the emanated etheric forms people naturally create through thought. We have already discussed how people naturally imprint their thoughts and ideas onto energy. In today's parlance, then, the term "thoughtform" usually refers to a thought which is intentionally given a form, such that the form can then be worked with energetically. Such a form can be empowered or weakened by energy and through correspondence to that which it represents. This is in effect a form of sympathetic magic, by which we perform the ritual or energetic working on one thing and through its associative link to the other, the effect is propagated to the actual target.

Though the term "form" would imply a shape, the shape is only important inasmuch as it carries symbolic meaning. A thoughtform is a shortcut towards a mechanical outcome in construct creation. A field that imprints boredom or disinterest in an object is simple enough, but through the use of thoughtforms we can program significantly more complicated processes or operations into our constructs. Step by step programming of a spell can become overly mechanical and thus distracting from simple, concise purpose. Earlier in the chapter on energetic cleaning and dissolution, we discussed a kind of construct that cleans a room. This also serves as an example of a thoughtform. We might, for example, create a construct that cleans our energetic field proceeding from the top to bottom while disposing of energy into salt left in a particular room, but this becomes quite a bit to go over and lends itself to distraction or lack of clarity.

The thoughtform of an energetic Roomba vacuum, however, carries all of the intended ideas with it, and needs only be directed for what it is cleaning. We have a clear enough idea of what an automatic vacuum robot does that the mere evocation of that symbolic idea is enough to create a functional construct when appropriately formed through energetic imprinting. Whereas earlier we had to take great care in the imprinting of a construct very specifically, by invoking the idea of a Roomba vacuum we can work around this, imbuing it with the behaviors via the shorthand of "what this is," and using the Roomba as a symbol.

Whereas the traditional ceremonial magician will invoke or evoke the thoughtforms or egregores with which he or she wishes to interact through ritual, the subtle energy manipulator does so through the direct programming and imprinting of energy. Via imprinting, physical objects can be made to house ideas and concepts, as we've already discussed. By employing more sophisticated egregores, we can pack more information into a single object or construct. Whereas the Roomba vacuum serves as a shorthand for the cleaning object, what if we wish to bring multiple functions into a single construct? Here we might build a construct which we wish to serve the purposes of a specific deity, a super hero, a character from fiction, whatever it is. If we need help finding lost things or solving problems, a construct programmed to function as a Sherlock Holmes may be a place to start. Of course, what we're accessing here is not the actual power of a fictional character, but rather an aspect of our own mind which holds the ideas about the great detective and delivers those to us in an energetic form.

When we build sophisticated energetic constructs which border on sentient through their robust functionality and through the programming of a personality, generally via the shortcut of imprinting an egregore or thoughtform, this is called a *servitor*. A lot of ethical debate goes into this issue, as a servitor is believed by some to be an actual sentient being, at least if it is sophisticated enough to exhibit those properties. When we create a construct to serve as a guardian angel or a protective spirit or the like, we enter a grey area from our own perception, as we see little difference between the subtle energetic bodies of such spirits and the constructs we've created. In this case I urge you to first consider how you feel about this, whether constructs can be sentient or not, before deciding to create ones that approach it. If they can, there are certainly moral and ethical considerations that must be weighed. If not, then it should not matter much. As your own ideas about this weigh heavily into the construction of such servitors, it is something you must decide for yourself.

INTERFACING WITH MAGIC: ELEMENTAL WORKING

As mentioned previously, the qualities of subtle energy can often be described by the alchemical elements related to the source from which it is drawn. We can of course use other qualifying descriptions; for example, what the energy is being used to accomplish, how it is imprinted, where it comes from, or so on. Why, then, would we want to characterize it in terms of alchemical elements? The answer here is simply to better interface with other magical systems. Many systems of magic write spells in terms of the elements being called upon, or draw up certain elements to enhance or diminish specific activities. By qualifying our energetic work in this way, we can interact with those magical workings in their own terms.

There are traditionally five classical alchemical elements in Western magic, these being earth, fire, water, wind, and quintessence, sometimes called "spirit." As mentioned before, all objects can be qualified in terms of their composition through these elements. Just as modern chemistry can determine the chemical composition of a thing, it is possible to determine the *alchemical* composition of a thing. Generally, this is done through looking at its sympathetic qualities.[19] In alchemy, a sympathetic relation is one that is attractive, and which supports a thing. Its opposite is antipathy, which interferes with something and drives it away. Properties that are sympathetic attract or sustain something, while antipathetic properties repel or diminish it.

A great deal of magic is related to these principles. Previously in this book, we used wards to attract or repel people, spirits, or so on. Now we see these properties again referring to objects or energies having favorable or unfavorable

---

[19] Sympathy as it relates to magic was previously discussed in the chapter on wards, here we see the concept developed further.

elements. In the classical alchemical elemental wheel, elements move towards their sympathies and oppose their antipathies. Thus, fire and water, earth and air stand opposed, while fire moves towards earth, earth towards water, water to air, and air to fire. In working with subtle energy, this can be used to interact with other magical workings or to inform or add a level of sophistication to our own creation of constructs. For example, to suppress anger and to promote patience and understanding in a room, we might ward it with general energetic fields of water, which will cool hot tempers, as well as air, which can facilitate communication; though we must take care with the latter as air can lead to fire. Or, working with another ritual, we might perform a Lesser Banishing Ritual of the Pentagram,[20] directing energetic movement around us concurrent to the direction of it through the ritual itself, thus adding an extra "layer" to the ritual.

As all objects possess elemental properties which are expressed in their nature, it can be said that all subtle energy possess elemental properties through imprinting. Before now, in this book, we have only worked with subtle energy in its unimprinted state, without paying attention to elemental properties. This is fine, as the use of subtle energy and its responsiveness to imprinting will generally remove energetic properties in the process of working with it. To work with these elemental properties instead, we can simply leave them in place, drawing the subtle energy we intend to work with from an object with those characteristics, or we can program it from our own energy, drawing the energy from the aspects of our bodies associated with each element. For example, we might draw air energy from our lungs, water from the blood, earth from the bone, and fire from the digestive organs. If we are working with

---

[20] A very common ritual developed by the Hermetic Order of the Golden Dawn which serves as a preliminary to all other workings within that ceremonial tradition, and is now used by many other schools derived from Golden Dawn materials.

this degree of precision, however, it becomes especially important that we are confident in our abilities and remain vigilant regarding our condition. While it has been stated that the subtle energy of the body is not something we are likely to exhaust, the mental idea of taking this energy from ourselves may give us the idea that we are reducing the amount of energy in, for example, our blood, and it is *this* idea that can cause us some harm. Even if we do not think about this at all, it is possible that we can hurt ourselves in this way, so it is included here more as an example of an idea than as a presentation of a particularly *good* idea. Instead, we can pull earth energy from the earth; water from any body of water, big or small; air energy from the wind or air around us; and fire energy from fire, the sun, or so on. This energy comes imprinted already, both by nature of association as well as by virtue of the collective egregore maintained about these sources.

In our own psychic workings, elemental properties can lend stronger associations. For telepathy, for example, the air element is excellent. For psychokinetic workings, earthy energy may be better. Water is cool and soothing, excellent for healing or empathic work; while fire can be used for aggressive or defensive work, or for causing agitation. Similarly, we can reduce these elements by removing or disenchanting them, bringing about the opposite effect. Taking the element of fire out of the energy in a room that is heavily agitated can calm it, whereas removing earth or water can destabilize it or lead to agitation. Taking the air out of a room can bring it down to earth, at the possible cost of communication. These energies can be drawn out, visualizing pulling them away until they are exhausted (and often directing them somewhere else, or grounding them away), or they can be depatternized and made to take on a new imprinting. It should be noted of course that energy that is depatternized or disenchanted will simply become re-imprinted with whatever is going on around it if left on its own, so depatternizing the energy in a room where a heated argument is taking place will likely only result in that energy being re-imprinted with the same hostile emotions, and taking on a yet fire-y elemental property.

Another way we can work with elements is using the Chinese elemental system of dynamic elements in the construction of elaborate psychic machines which function on process and movement of transformation, rather than focusing directly on compositing the construct. Whereas we might build a construct that has certain properties which we can employ using the Western alchemical elements, the Chinese elements provide a sophisticated system of dynamic interaction which can be used to create constructs which move through various processes. The resultant construct will be more oriented towards undergoing a process rather than being a static object, which is itself an important consideration for more advanced construct creation. Whereas most are inclined to energetically program a construct which is a *thing*, a *noun*, and which thing then goes about performing an action, there is no reason why we cannot develop a construct which is itself a *process*, a *verb*.

Approached this way, the construct will perform its task more efficiently and effectively, with less effort spent on developing the "how" of the desired task, and more effort spent on actually performing the task itself. Taking as an example our energetic cleaning Roomba, we may not want to focus so much on building a construct which cleans, and so waste effort in the design of an enduring, remaining energetic object which performs a task, when in this case we can simply program into existence a construct which is itself "cleaning."

As it is not strictly related to energy work, a discussion of both the Western alchemical and Chinese elemental systems is included in Appendix C of this book.

BEYOND TECHNIQUE

I wrote this book as an update to a previous book I had written, but also to fill a need in the magical and psychic community for introductory material that did not merely deliver rote lists of steps to follow, but also a firm philosophical basis on which someone could develop and build their magical or psychic practice, or augment their already existing practice. Much of the contents of this book are not new, but are presented here in a new way which I believe leaves the reader with a better command of the information as well as the ability to discuss, compare, and contrast direct subtle energy manipulation with other magical systems one is likely to encounter, and to perform at some level a wide variety of psychic feats traditionally thought to belong only to the rare natural psychic. By diligently practicing the material in this book, the reader will have become a capable and competent user of subtle energy.

We have covered in this book a variety of topics from the very basic and rudimentary imprinting of objects to healing to more traditionally "psychic" skills like telepathy, empathy, clairvoyance, and the like. These skills have been presented in brief "how-to" style approaches, rather than enumerating a wide number of uses and applications. How you can use these abilities in your life is something of an exercise for the reader. Many practitioners of subtle energy work may list out a great number of uses, and many will have *different* uses.

Instead of providing in this book a list of solutions to problems, I have opted to focus on giving you a set of tools. How you use those tools is for you to decide. It is not necessary to follow rigidly or dogmatically the instructions of any energy worker in specific. Different methods work well for different people, and even within this book I have at times presented different approaches. Do not stick with my methods when others may work better, and do not feel limited to using shields, wards, telepathy, or anything in this book in a certain prescribed way. Experiment! What others may say does not work, might work very well for you.

Having explored and mastered the material in this book, an aspiring student may be wondering where to go next. It is my suggestion that anyone with an interest in subtle energy work itself most likely also has an interest in the magical traditions of any number of spiritual traditions, and should consider strongly pursuing one of those. Subtle energy work can be used to benefit others and oneself, but it does not bring us spiritual fulfillment or particularly great benefits, and it works best in conjunction with, rather than in lieu of, other, more traditional magical approaches. We should not limit ourselves strictly to working with subtle energy as even if what some people insist is true, and magical work merely mobilizes subtle energies, there is something to the psychological component of more concrete magical work that imparts a certain power on a work.

Those who prefer to stick with the sterile secular approaches may instead explore radionics, a kind of magic that works with subtle energy and interfaces it with technology. Instead of an altar, the radionic magician builds a workstation out of switches and dials and works his or her intent through the interface of technology rather than through the interface of religion. Additionally, those inclined towards clairvoyance may be interested in remote viewing, a protocol driven method for obtaining information about targets through anomalous means and developed by Stanford Research Institute and the Department of Defense, Defense Intelligence Agency, and other American intelligence agencies in the 1970s, '80s, and '90s. While these disciplines are not strictly related, people interested purely in secular magic and psychicism often find that remote viewing training can provide the incontrovertible proof of the reality of psychic phenomena that they have been seeking.

Whatever it is you prefer, there are a great number of resources on more specialized applications of subtle energy applications often termed "psionics" or "psychic energy work" available which go into more depth than this book has covered. As stated, this book has served you as an introduction to the field married with practical advice on cultivating skills to obtain results through subtle energy. As an introduction, it has not gone too far into depth on many things. But I will remind you that it is this foundation on which you yourself can build. With these strong fundamentals, you can explore your own path forward, inventing and developing techniques as necessary by assembling the techniques provided here like building blocks.

A shield or ward can be anchored to a construct, or a construct can be used as a roving eye to assist clairvoyance, or as a notifier when people have approached its "line of sight." It can heal or harm those that approach it, and so on. While it is good to study further and learn more about the skills which interest you most, do not mistake this book's introductory foundational nature for being *ineffective*. Your application of the concepts in this book will have already made you a competent subtle energy worker ready to launch into the occult world able to walk and run already, and now it is your turn to explore.

I should mention finally that it is my belief that the most important skill discussed in this book is the first one, that of meditation. It is through meditation that we develop the mental faculties that can really help us in our daily lives. This book does not teach advanced meditation of the sort that can really benefit a person, but even the very simple meditation taught here can have real and tangible effects on our lives. If there is nothing else to take home from this book, it should be that mindfulness and a tamed mind are the greatest tools we possess towards accomplishing *any* task, not merely psychic ones. If you pursue nothing else from this book in your studies, let it be the practice of meditation that you seek out more information on. Everything else you can develop on your own, but to really progress in meditation will require a qualified spiritual master to instruct you, and I am not that person.

APPENDIX A: CHAKRAS AND ENERGY CENTERS

There are in fact many sorts of systems of classification and formal instruction regarding the energetic focal centers in the body we commonly refer to as chakras. By far the most popular system of chakra classification in use today is the seven chakra system popularized with the Theosophical Society by C.W. Leadbeater, who translated a Sanskrit text from the 16th century as his primary and definitive source. This system, notably, was itself largely innovative and not part of any ancient tantric tradition. Regardless of the lack of ancient provenance, the system is now largely widespread, having disseminated from East to West, and from West back to East, such that it enjoys widespread popularity in yoga circles and New Age philosophy alike. Because of this pervasiveness it would be a disservice to not speak to the various energetic systems in the body as described by this system.

It should only be kept in mind that this is a conceptual model, not an anatomical reality. These chakras can be considered to have a function in the interrelations of the energy bodies as described in that chapter, but they exist because those functions exist and so we can form a symbolic representation of that function in working with energy.

In the seven chakra system, the chakras progress from the root chakra along the central channel to the crown chakra, running through the body roughly along the spine. Each chakra is generally iconically represented by a lotus flower with a varying number of petals upon each of which are written Sanskrit syllables which traditionally represent elements in tantra and correspond to the associated deity. In the modern use, these syllables are held to represent or associate with the chakra themselves. Each chakra has a conventional English name as well as a traditional Sanskrit name. In certain exercises, energy is brought progressively from the root chakra up through the crown, and the ascendency and operationality of this energy is said to unlock various energetic abilities. It should be noted that there are significant risks involved in working with this energy and process, called *kundalini*, so much so that the American Psychiatric Association's *Diagnostic and Statistical Manual of Mental Disorders, 4th Ed.* Recognized "kundalini syndrome" as a complex of psychiatric disturbances resultant from untrained and reckless work with kundalini outside of a regimented training process. Unless you are a yogi working with a proper guru, I would strongly discourage that kind of work.

Chakras in this system are often said to be balanced or imbalanced, with balanced chakras resulting in their positive associated manifestations and imbalanced chakras resulting in the associated neuroses or anxieties. As a model for energetic healing, therefore, the chakra system is as good a symbol set as any to work with. The following overview is entirely superficial and serves only as a brief summary for readers unfamiliar with the system. To really understand how this system works, you could ask almost any modern yoga practitioner, or research the subject in more depth through books and so on.

The root chakra, or *muladhara*, is located at the end of the tailbone, on the seat when sitting in the lotus posture, and is associated with stability, groundedness, and security. It is represented by a red lotus of four petals. Unbalance here is often associated with anxiety or nervousness and particularly with insecurity. It is the anchor point of the etheric body and the energetic body, and represents the interconnection between the two. When we need to emphasize our physical being in our physical body, we can center to this chakra, drawing energy out of it and imprinting our field with it to correct the etheric field to the physical body's state.

Proceeding upward, the sacral chakra or *svadisthana* is located approximately four finger-widths below the navel, and is represented by an orange lotus of six petals, it symbolizes the sexual and creative energies of a person. We draw energy from this chakra when working with subtle energy not for its association with this chakra system but because that same center is regarded in other energetic traditions as the storehouse or base of bodily energy or heat. The sacral chakra is the intersection of the etheric and emotional bodies. When we are disturbed emotionally, we can first find our calm, and then center to this chakra. The energy body will imprint with our negative emotions and keep us feeling badly for a long time if it is not reset, so centering to this chakra is helpful after we have calmed ourselves down physically.

The solar plexus chakra, *manipura*, is located at the solar plexus, represented by a yellow lotus of ten petals. It represents individual will and personal power, and is also commonly used by energy workers as the chakra which mobilizes energy. The process by which most energy workers familiar with chakras operate is to draw from the root or sacral chakra, proceeding to the solar chakra, and then being set in motion from there. The solar plexus chakra represents the mental-astral form of personal ego-identity, what Rudolf Steiner calls the ego-self. Centering on the solar plexus is particularly useful for telepaths and empaths who are being overwhelmed and "lost" in other people's thoughts and emotions. An empath who has lost his or her sense of self and is caught up in someone else's emotions can center here to return to his or her own emotional channel. A telepath who has lost his or her own mental voice in the din of thoughts arising can use this to find his or her own "stream of consciousness" again.

The heart chakra, *anahata*, is located in the center of the chest and is represented by a green lotus of twelve petals. It represents universal love in the modern tradition, and often represents the mind or spiritual center in other systems. It is the focus of meditation when engaging in certain forms of yoga for the cultivation of love and interconnectedness. This link with love and compassion is also related to its function as a mediator of emotional interaction with others in the mental astral body. It serves to represent our compassion for others. We can center here when we are caught up in negative emotions towards others.

The throat chakra, or *vissudha*, is located at the throat, with a blue lotus of sixteen petals as its representation. It represents communication and sometimes is associated with telepathy, though usually it is associated with conventional speech and conventional exchange between beings. It represents the astral body as it pertains to communication. If we are having difficulty communicating, either understanding others or making ourselves understood, centering here can help us organize our thoughts for communication.

The third eye, *anja*, is located on the forehead just between the eyebrows. It is represented usually by a purple lotus with two petals, or more simply by an eye. The third eye generally represents intuition and perception of energy and the astral planes. It is a focus of meditation in cultivating astral senses. These kinds of meditations are effective because of the strong association between the third eye and this kind of extra-sensory perception, and demonstrates the strength of culturally transmitted symbols in self transformation using subtle energy. It is also commonly associated with telepathic and clairvoyant functionality. Naturally, it represents the astral body as it pertains to perception and sensitivity. When we're insensitive or having a hard time organizing our perceptions, or when our psychic senses have been scrambled by exposure to depatternizing fields or other psychic harm, centering here can help restore these intuitive faculties.

The crown chakra, *sahasrara*, is located on the crown of the head, opening outward from the body, a violet colored lotus of twelve (or infinite) petals which open to the expanse. It represents universal consciousness or contact with the divine in the modern tradition, and so is sometimes related to clairvoyance or remote viewing type applications, as well as astral projection and so on. It represents the astral body's connection to the greater domain of all things, and so it is used in mystic experiences and experiences of interconnectedness. Problems with astral projection or with feeling closed in and disconnected from the world can be addressed by centering here.

In lieu of considering these to be actual structures within the energetic anatomy, they should be considered as conceptual structures which arise out of various functions and intersections of the energetic body. For example, the root chakra affects the physical body and serves as the intersection point of the physical and etheric bodies. It exists because we can conceive of that functional point. When we instantiate it as a chakra, it allows us to work with this intersection through visualization exercises or inner work. Likewise, the sacral and heart chakras can be conceived of as the intersection of the emotional-astral and physical bodies.

In our discussion of the energetic anatomy, we mentioned that the mental-astral body corresponds with the third eye chakra, though in truth it corresponds with many chakras dependent on function. The chakras can be considered to serve different cognitive functions, as described before. The third eye represents our ability to perceive and our interaction with mental-forms. The crown chakra connects us to the universe in a non-dual way. The heart chakra regulates emotional thinking, the solar plexus regulates volition and will. In the more sophisticated theosophically-derived models, the solar plexus would correspond with the *causal body*, the third eye with the *mental body*, and so on.

These chakras can be used through energetic focus, charging, and meditation based on their associations in the modern tradition fairly easily, although it would be prudent to seek out much more instruction and information than can be found here before doing so. Because these are ubiquitous structures in yogic and new age circles, they are generally well understood. What is important is to bear in mind that these are not structures that exist prior to the formations of these intersections. That is, we do not first have a solar plexus chakra, and from that gain a causal body and volition. They are not mechanical structures, but rather organically arising ways of categorizing activities which occur within the energy field. When we look at the "solar plexus chakra," what we are looking for are the elements of the energetic field that resemble the formation of volition, will, ego, and self-assertion. When we look at the "heart chakra," what we are looking at is the organized conceptualization of compassion.

Steiner asserts that these chakras "awaken" through spiritual practice and that this can be observed by the spiritual teacher. I think that this observation is certainly possible, but not because the chakra is dormant and then awakens. Instead, the chakra as a *concept* becomes more apparent when we look for the characteristics that correspond to it. The structure does not necessarily exist, but it is a way for our own minds to organize the functions of the astral body in a format we can make sense of.

Again, this is merely a brief discussion for the purpose of familiarization with concepts that you are likely to have already encountered or almost certainly will encounter, but which have been largely omitted from this book in order to reduce the tendency to force the reader into a particular set of assumptions or spiritual paths.

APPENDIX B: ON HERMETIC PHILOSOPHY IN THIS BOOK

Throughout this book I make references to Hermetic philosophy. It is important to note that this is not a book about Hermeticism, and the application here is not part of Hermetic orthodoxy. Nevertheless, the topics discussed are related to Hermeticism just as much of the Western esoteric tradition generally is related to Hermetic thought. Hermeticism is a philosophy popularized in the 1300s and claiming a much greater and older heritage as the first philosophy of everything from which all philosophical and religious doctrines are derived, named for the philosopher Hermes Trismegistus to whom all Hermetic texts are credited. The oldest body of Hermetic philosophy, the *Hermetica*, and specifically the *Emerald Tablet* which names Hermes Trismegistus, date to around the 2nd century CE. The philosophy is summarized in the much more recent text, the *Kybalion*, which was published in 1907 and claims to be authored by the "three initiates" who have carried the Hermetic teachings forward.

The body of Hermetic philosophy is vast, comprising in itself a complete mystical initiatic system as well as a system of alchemy, astrology, and theurgy. Numerous texts have been written since the *Emerald Tablet*, and many extremely popular texts, such as the *Three Books of Occult Philosophy,* by Heinrich Cornelius Agrippa, enumerate in substantive detail a great number of practices and ideas. These texts include books on the aforementioned practices of astrology and alchemy, about natural science, about the nature of planets, spirits, intelligences, plants, medicine, and so on. It is far too vast for me to go into it in detail. However, two topics are referenced somewhat extensively in the later parts of this book which deserve some elaboration.

Firstly, Hermetic philosophy provides a cosmology of three "planes" which comprise the universe of experience: the physical plane, which we inhabit; the astral plane, which is the subtle plane where spirits live and the home of the noumena, things as they actually are; and the mental plane, which is made of our concepts, thoughts, and ideas, and serves as an intersection of our mental interaction with other planes. The Theosophical society which later adopted many Hermetic ideas as their own also interjected the etheric plane, which is a coarser plane which interfaces between the astral and the physical.

In both cases, the concepts of these planes are vague and philosophical, and a real understanding of them is only possible within the context of the greater philosophies in which they are found. In this book, I have provided deliberately little detail as dogmatic adherence to certain traditions or styles is somewhat contrary to the purpose of this work. In all modern Western magical traditions I can think of, these three or four planes exist in some form or another, their characteristics slightly different but their general functions the same. If you are an adherent to one of these traditions, you can certainly ascribe to the planes your system's beliefs. If you are not an adherent, then enough detail has been provided for you to functionally work with the planes, and your understanding of them will expand by experience.

One thing that must be understood however is that these planes exist relationally to one another. The astral and the physical planes reflect one another, according to a principle of Hermetic philosophy called "Correspondence." The Principle of Correspondence is summarized "as above, so below." This correspondence is seen in all interactions. It represents the correspondence of the macrocosm to the microcosm, but also the correspondence of the astral to the material, the mental to the astral, the mental to the material, and so on. This understanding of "as above, so below" is how much of Western esotericism goes about influencing the material world. For example, the magician performs a ritual in the material world, which has an astral consequence. These changes on the astral then have an impact on the material world. It is this correspondence that allows astral activities to affect the material, and material actions to affect the astral. Much of Western magic is contingent upon this understanding, and as this text makes an effort to provide a system of subtle energy manipulation which is compatible, rather than competitive, with ritual magic across cultures, it is necessary to introduce this concept.

There are seven principles of Hermetic philosophy outlined in the Kybalion, which I will briefly describe here. A more in depth study could and should be made by the aspiring Hermeticist, but for the purposes of informing the reader, I offer this brief list of descriptions:

1) The Principle of Mentalism: "All is Mind," declares the Kybalion. This principle demonstrates the idea that all phenomenal experience proceeds from mind, rather than preceding from mind. Any mental phenomena or experience arises as a result of the preceding mental state, rather than the other way around. When we experience something, it is because prior to the experience, we mentally disposed ourselves to it.

2) The Principle of Correspondence: "As above, so below." This has already been covered in some detail, but it expands into the three spheres of experience in the assertion that whatever occurs in one plane (material, mental, astral or physical, emotional, mental) occurs in the other planes as well in some form or another. Additionally, it refers to the microcosm and macrocosm, wherein each person contains within themselves a complete system of cosmogony which mirrors that of the external universe, the two mutually coarisen and inseparable.

3) The Principle of Vibration: Everything is moving, vibrating, or spinning in relation to everything else. One vibration one place is communicated to

everywhere else. Nothing stays still or is stagnant, but everything, even things which are seemingly at rest, are subtly moving, changing, and relating to the world around.

4) The Principle of Polarity: everything has its own state and its opposite state simultaneously. A front necessitates a back, an up necessitates a down. Existence necessitates non-existence, and everything that exists also at once possesses the characteristic of not-existing.

5) The Principle of Rhythm: from understanding polarity, there is also a rhythm, a back and forth movement from state to state. Things move according to rhythms and things cycle through their own phases in their own times.

6) The Principle of Cause and Effect: no result arises without a cause; no cause exists without a result. Everything that occurs occurs dependent on something else, everything that is done results in something else.

7) The Principle of Gender: unrelated to the concepts of biological or mental gender, but rather related to the concept of creation. All the universe, through the synthesis of the previous principles, is in a constant state of creation and recreation, serving to create either through masculine or feminine principles. Here, femininity refers to the creative elements of reception, and masculinity to the creative elements of expression. Everything is, at once, becoming, either through reception of or expression of change.

These principles comprise a robust philosophical and mystical system which is used by varying traditions towards various goals, be it apotheosis, enlightenment, ego-abnegation, spiritual alchemy, or so on. More mundanely, these principles inform the magician. By recognizing these principles as present in all phenomena, the magician, psychic, or sorcerer can see how to push them in order to achieve the goals they aim for. It is not the purpose of this book to present a Hermetic approach to magic, but at least within the discussion of the planes and the application of subtle energy work across planes, as well as within the use of subtle energy as it relates to elements, there is some value in familiarity with the concepts, if not utter reliance on them.

APPENDIX C: ON ALCHEMICAL ELEMENTS

The classical alchemical elements have their own correspondences which are discussed in some detail in many texts and which are the subject of treatises and so on. The properties of the elements themselves, as well as their functions and relations, are the subject of considerable study. Because the elements are found in all things, there are long lists of sympathies and antipathies regarding various plants, minerals, metals, and so on. Learning these properties gives a general understanding of the elements themselves, and their alchemical significance.

Strictly speaking, within the Western alchemical system, there are four material elements, and quintessence. The four material elements are earth, water, air, and fire, and display the properties of cool, hot, dry, and moist. Fire is hot and dry, earth is cool and dry, water is cool and moist, and air is hot and moist. These words carry with them additional meanings, however, in that hot elements are ascending or expansive, while cool elements are descending. Dry elements are rigid, while moist elements are fluid.

The cool elements, earth and water, always seek a lowest point. They will descend, rather than rising. The hot elements rise, ascending or climbing. Moist elements conform to the shape of the vessel they are in. Dry elements maintain their own shape. Fire, in this last case, only travels along the surfaces of objects and so can be said to hold the shape of the object it is consuming.

So, in looking at the properties of elements, we can get a feeling for their general tendencies. Earth is cool and dry, so it is static and solid. Once molded, it does not change shape on its own. It has a great amount of inertia, and is not "consumed" through use. This element might be employed when we are trying to make something very solid, a long lasting construct, for example, or if we're attempting to accomplish something very sympathetic to the material. Symbolically, it represents materiality and physicality, as well as material and physical concerns like money or finances. It is associated with the coins of the Tarot, or the Pentacle on a ceremonial altar.

Water is cool and moist. Like earth, it descends, but unlike earth, water withdraws inward. Earth falls to the lowest point, but water seeps through the cracks, inward and deep. It is moist, instead of dry, so it conforms to whatever vessel it is placed in but does not hold its own shape well. Watery elemental energies are soothing and cool, pacifying, but they are not particularly good for holding their shape, and so do not make good rigid constructs. Symbolically, water is the feminine aspect of receiving, as well as emotion and social events. It is associated with the Cups of the Tarot as well as the Chalice on the ceremonial altar.

Air is hot and moist, and above all it is expansive. Whereas water seeps and sinks to fill the vessels it is placed in, air expand and rises to fill the same vessels. It escapes upwards, rather than by seeping downwards. Air is the least rigid, with neither its descendant nature nor rigidity to hold it in place. Whereas earth is the most static element, air is the most dynamic. Air is symbolized in the Tarot by the Sword, and its ceremonial tool is the athame or dagger.

Fire is hot and dry. Though it is expansive, it does not spread off of the rigid form of its fuel, and so maintains a rough shape of its fuel. It does have the impetus to rise. Fire is primarily transformative and agitating, it is the most reactive of the alchemical elements. The introduction of fire into a process accelerates it and increases vibration. Where water is the receptive female, fire the male creative element of expression. Its Tarot association is the baton, and its ceremonial tool is the wand.

All objects can be considered comprised by these elements and determining their rough proportions within an object are a function of identifying their characteristics based on these properties. The interactions of the elements in objects are as we can expect; for example, excessively dry things are antipathetic to wet things, sympathetic to dry things.

Spirits, too, are comprised of elements and their characteristics are likewise correspondent. Traditionally, each element has a family of elemental spirits associated with it. Earth elementals are called gnomes, and generally live in subterranean spaces but in some cultures they are also understood to function as helping spirits within homes ("house elves" or "kobolds"). Fire elementals, called salamanders, resemble their biological homonym in shape and color but bear little other resemblance. They are not amphibious. In some cultures, these elementals also take on humanoid characteristics, resembling djinns. Air elementals, called sylphs, have transient and amorphous forms. Their form resembles cirrus clouds, wispy and wind-blown, and they do not stay still unless they are forced into a container, instead moving freely through the skies. Water elementals are called undines, and their forms tend to be those of female humanoid or mermaids.

In iconography and symbolism, undines, gnomes, and sylphs will all take on humanoid forms or shapes. Gnomes are usually short humans, undines appear as virginal youths in bodies of water, and sylphs appear as typical fairies, with lacy wings and so on, albeit normal human sized (these are notably distinct from fairies in folklore and mythology). Salamanders, on the other hand, are almost always represented as fire-breathing lizards roughly the size of a medium dog or Komodo dragon.

These elementals all find their own elements sympathetic and it is not unheard of for people working with elemental energies to encounter such spirits. This contact can be established telepathically, or through some form of the elemental focus, or the sudden appearance of the correspondent elements. In some cases, people will specifically call on the elementals to assist in elemental work, following the idea that naturally these spirits will be more adept at manipulating their energies than others.

Elemental Modes

Each element also has a mode, or system of functioning. This is most evident in the quadruplicities of Western and Vedic astrology, but can be useful for our understanding of the different functions elements can serve within a system. Each element can be found in cardinal, fixed, or mutable *modes*, which describe the characteristics of the element itself.

The cardinal mode is that of initiation of processes and beginnings. It is also the "action" form of an element, characterizing that element's activity. The fixed mode is the rigid form of an element, or that element in its resting state. The mutable mode is the characteristic of the element in its transitional state, either moving from cardinal to fixed, fixed to cardinal, or more commonly transitioning into another element altogether. For each element, the mode affects how it is functioning within a system.

For fire, the cardinal expression is that of an incipient flame, the growth of the fire from a match light to a roaring forest fire. The fixed form is that of the sun, or other glowing and radiating processes which do not necessarily involve the burning process of fire. In a mutable mode, fire is directed in transformative activity, something like a laser cutter, or else it is transforming into another element or mode, or its transformative function of one element into another through burning. In astrology, the cardinal, fixed, and mutable expressions of fire are Aries, Leo, and Sagittarius, respectively.

Earth's cardinal expression is that of construction and building, establishing things firmly, and performing earthworks. The fixed function is that of the unmoving mountain, strong and stable. In its mutable mode, Earth is the transformation of other elements or the transition of fluid systems into solid ones, like the hardening of concrete, and the transformative process of crushing or molding. Astrologically, the cardinal, fixed, and mutable modes are Capricorn, Taurus, and Virgo.

Water's cardinal expression is that of nurturing and cultivation. Here we are not as interested in water as a body of water, but as a womb, or as a necessary component for growth. Water in its cardinal expression nourishes. The fixed position of water is one of descent. The "wet" elements do not "fix" well, but rather they take the shape of whatever vessel they are in. Water descends to do so, it searches the depths. The mutable position of water is that of flowing and transition, the process of freezing and melting, and the transformative effect of water in dissolving other things. Astrologically the cardinal, fixed, and mutable modes of water are Cancer, Scorpio, and Pisces respectively.

For air, the cardinal expression is that of the whirlwind or the headwind, carrying things along in a certain direction. Wind behind our sails carry us forward, and this is the cardinal expression of wind. Symbolically air is associated with intellectual pursuits, and so this can be a strong element for working with knowledge. Notably, this element's cardinal mode seems better for inducing action in others. The fixed expression of air is pressure resisting expansion, air inside a container which wants to expand out. The mutable expression is that of its conformity to shapes it finds itself in, and the transformation of other elements through abrasion (like a pressure washer) or movement. Astrologically the cardinal, fixed, and mutable modes are Libra, Aquarius, and Gemini respectively.

Eastern Systems of Elements

The Western model of the elements is only one perspective on the constituent elements of things. In addition to the Western model, there is also the Vedic system from India, which is composed of the same elements as the West but with Space (dimensionality) in the place of quintessence, and a slightly different understanding of the characteristics of each element. Space as an element is unique because it is an element which underlies all other elements. For there to be fire, there must be space. So on with each other element. Additionally, while other elements interact or can even be destroyed or changed through that interaction, space itself as an element does not change and is not affected by whatever exists within it. If you fill a room with boxes, it does not change the volume of the room itself. Because the other elements themselves remain mostly the same, we'll not spend much time on the Vedic system.

The Chinese, however, have a much different system of elemental working and it is something that is worth being familiar with even if one does not intend to work with Chinese elements if only because the philosophy of it emphasizes dynamism rather than static configurations and this is worthy of consideration in our own magical or elemental workings.

In the Chinese elemental system, the five elements are wood, fire, earth, iron, and water. While it is tempting to try to correspond these to the Western or Vedic elements, we must suppress that temptation, because these five elements are not understood in a static way, each with their own characteristics. Unlike the Western system, for example, Chinese elemental "water" is not defined terms of being "wet and cool," for example, but rather in its relationship to the other elements.

Each element is defined in terms of its relationship, and that relationship tells us what sympathies and antipathies there are and what interactions will occur. So, all elements are characterized by their mother, child, friend, and enemy. The mother is the most sympathetic element, which nurtures and nourishes its child. The child, in turn, pulls from the mother, gaining power from its mother. The child is strongly sympathetic to the mother, and the mother is neutral to the child. The friend is the element which an element dominates, and the enemy is the element which dominates another element. Each element is weakly sympathetic to its friend, and strongly antipathetic to its enemy.

Another way, we can understand the mother to be the cause or basis of something, a child to be the result of something, the friend to be what something destroys, and the enemy to be that which destroys something.

So, starting in order, wood's mother is water, its child is fire, its friend is earth, and its enemy is iron. Water nourishes wood and encourages its growth. Fire burns with wood as the cause. Wood grows through the earth, destroying it, and wood is chopped down by iron.

Fire's mother is wood, its child earth, its friend iron, and its enemy water. Fire arises on the basis of wood as the fuel. As it burns, it becomes ash, which is earth. With fire we can melt iron, and of course water extinguishes fire.

Earth's mother is fire, its child is iron, its friend water, and its enemy wood. Earth results from the fire. We mine iron from earth. Soil sucks up water and water cannot be recovered from it, and it is destroyed by growth (picture here a tree which as it has grown splits a rock in half).

Iron's mother is earth, its child water, its friend is wood and its enemy fire. We mine iron from the earth. Water condenses and arises on the surface of iron. Iron easily chops wood, but it is melted and becomes soft when exposed to fire.

Water's mother is iron, its child wood, its friend fire and its enemy earth. Here, we see water condenses and forms on iron in the morning. From water, wood can grow. Its friend is the fire which it can easily extinguish, and its enemy is the earth which can soak it up and absorb it.

When we arrange these elements in order around the points of a pentagram, the relationship follows: from wood, the mother relations rotate clockwise, the child relations rotate anticlockwise. The friend relations move in a clockwise star, and the enemy relations follow the same star anticlockwise. The clockwise relations are sympathetic, and the anticlockwise relations are antipathetic (enemies) or neutral (children).

Appendix D: Psychokinesis

Psychokinesis is perhaps one of the most difficult abilities to gain even a passable competence in, and the energetic approach to this effect is perhaps even more so. I will preface here that I am by no means an expert on psychokinesis as such. It has never been a focus of my attention and I am not very good at it. That said, it is one of the most sought after abilities and it would be neglectful of me to not address it at all.

Psychokinesis comes in two different forms, generally termed Micro-PK and Macro-PK. The former is essentially probability manipulation, and refers to psychically influencing random outcomes to make them slightly less random. Usually used with random number generators under experimental conditions, there are of course other applications for this ability. Micro-PK would also refer to subtle alterations to already-in-process events, where a very small influence can bring about a physical change. This would include, for example, trying to manipulate the landing of dice that are already being thrown, or trying to stack a deck of cards. Macro-PK is what most people think of when they hear the term "psychokinesis," and refers to the dramatic and undeniable ability to move physical objects about with the mind. Both abilities can be seen innately or through spiritual attainments of the sort demonstrated by yogis or accomplished mystics, but both can also be learned through direct energy manipulation, albeit at great cost of time in the case of Macro-PK.

Micro-PK is easy enough to bring about for reasons we've already discussed earlier. Manipulating probabilities and outcomes can be easily accomplished merely using a construct. This is the simplest way to go about affecting the result we desire. From the working state, simply reach out energetically and, making contact with the object or outcome you wish to influence, create a construct that imposes the desired outcome. Charging that construct with energy to bring about its affect, or directly altering the target's astral signature to bring about the effect through correspondence, is all that really needs to be done here. Done properly, it is likely you can bring about a statistically significant effect with little effort. That said, dramatic 100% certain effects on random number generators are very difficult to attain as the equipment is usually built to prevent this. Computer based random number generators often use a kind of simulated randomness, the seed is predictable but the likelihood of influencing the output with 100% effectiveness is very low. It is important not to become discouraged over statistically significant successes that do not come to absolute efficacy; that path leads to madness.

Another technique for Micro-PK is similar to a technique for Macro-PK, and involves a bit more mental exercise. This essentially involves recognizing the object as not separate from, or other than, yourself. Once the target is firmly identified as inseparable from or part of yourself, visualize the outcome coming about the way you would visualize moving your own limbs if you were planning a complicated physical feat. Feel the object move as if you were moving your own body, or, in this case, feel yourself generating the desired effect or outcome. I find this solution particularly effective when interacting with physical systems, throwing the dice as an extension of myself where I land them with whatever number I need, or shuffling a deck of cards in such a way as to be in the order I'd like.

For Macro-PK, both processes are similar. Here, an energetic effect can be used as well, with a strong programming on the object's own energetic field imprinting that the object is in motion. Done both physically and astrally, this will hopefully correspond to it actually coming to pass. Doing so requires a significant expenditure of energy, however, and is not without biological repercussions. Famed Russian psychokinetic Nina Kulagina suffered a heart attack in the late 1970s after performing extensively for Soviet researchers. Even for her, a natural psychokinetic, performing PK took considerable energy, effort, and time. Her methodology involved more of a meditative stillness, a focus of the mind without distraction and with total concentration. Alternatively to the purely energetic method, some psychokinetics use the method of recognizing of the object as an extension of oneself, then moving the object as if moving one's own body.

Typically, Micro-PK can be practiced using any kind of random number generating system. Electronic systems seemingly tend to be easier to interact with, so online dice rollers or random number generators can work, although for reasons mentioned before, without an actually genuinely random seed, they can be very hard to work with. For Macro-PK, the "psi-wheel," or "psychic pinwheel," has been the historically most popular tool. Taking a piece of tinfoil or paper and folding it into a pinwheel configuration, place it on the point of a pin or toothpick or so on. Place this under some kind of glass cover, so as to prevent your own breath from moving the object and unwittingly defrauding yourself. Then proceed to practice, attempting to make the pinwheel spin or rotate, using the techniques detailed above.

Unfortunately, psychokinesis generally, and especially macro-PK, has never been a particularly strong skill of mine, and is difficult to teach even for very experienced people. If this is the primary focus of one's studies, the above is merely offered to help familiarize oneself with the basic processes before moving into a much more detailed study. One should be prepared to spend many hours per day working on this skill until they "get" it, and then still a significant amount of time practicing even after this. If you do choose to pursue this, it is advised to practice in short sessions rather than in long continuous sessions. The strain on one's body can be quite significant, and long, continuous sessions are a contributing factor.

Further Reading

Broughton, R.S. (1991). *Parapsychology: the controversial science*. New York, NY: Ballantine Books.

Butler, W.E. (1998). *How to read the aura: And practice psychometry, telepathy, & clairvoyance*. Rochester, VT: Destiny Books.

Leadbeater, C.W. (2009). *The chakras*. Anand Gholap Theosophical Institute.

Mishlove, J. (1988). *PSI development systems*. New York, NY: Ballantine Books

Miller, K. (2019). *Subtle spirits: A handbook of spirits and mediumship*. Frederick, MD: Turtles and Crows.

Miller, R.M., & Harper, J.M. (1987). *The psychic energy workbook*.

Naparstek, B. (1998). *Your sixth sense: Unlocking the power of your intuition*. New York: Harper One.

Puharich, A. (1973). *Beyond telepathy*. Garden City, NY; Anchor Press.

Sadowski, E.R. (2017). *Intuition and intuition development: Practices for the inner self* (Unpublished doctoral thesis). Retrieved from http://summit.sfu.ca/item/17780

Silva, J. (1977). *The Silva mind control method.* New York, NY: Pocket Books.

Steiner, R. (1909). *Initiation and its results*. Retrieved from https://wn.rsarchive.org/Books/GA010/English/MAC1909/GA010b_index.html

Stevenson, I. (1970). *Telepathic impressions: A review and report of 35 new cases*. Charlottesville, VA: University Press of Virginia.

Tamphel, K., Trans. (2010). Shamatha to mahamudra. New Delhi, India: Archana Press.

Vaughan, F.E. (1979). *Awakening intuition*. New York: Anchor Books.

ABOUT THE AUTHOR

Keith Miller is a psychic and a lifelong student of the paranormal. He holds a master's degree in transpersonal psychology from Atlantic University. In addition to parapsychology and the paranormal, he has studied a wide range of occult topics, including Western and Tibetan astrology, divination, card reading, and radionics.

The author of several books on paranormal topics, Keith is also a teacher and lecturer. By studying methods of psi development from around the world, he has developed a systematic, step-by-step method of psychic ability development.

Printed in Great Britain
by Amazon